A MARINER'S GUIDE TO SELF SABOTAGE

BILL GASTON

STORIES

A MARINER'S GUIDE TO

SELF SABOTAGE

Douglas & McIntyre

COPYRIGHT © 2017 BILL GASTON
1 2 3 4 5 — 21 20 19 18 17

All rights reserved. No part of this publication may be reproduced, stored in a retrieval system or transmitted, in any form or by any means, without prior permission of the publisher or, in the case of photocopying or other reprographic copying, a licence from Access Copyright, www.accesscopyright.ca, 1-800-893-5777, info@accesscopyright.ca.

DOUGLAS AND MCINTYRE (2013) LTD.
P.O. Box 219, Madeira Park, BC, V0N 2H0
www.douglas-mcintyre.com

Edited by Barbara Berson
Cover photograph by Kristopher Roller
Cover design by Anna Comfort O'Keeffe
Text design by Shed Simas / Onça Design
Printed and bound in Canada
Printed on paper made from 100% post-consumer waste

DOUGLAS AND MCINTYRE (2013) LTD. acknowledges the support of the Canada Council for the Arts, which last year invested $153 million to bring the arts to Canadians throughout the country. We also gratefully acknowledge financial support from the Government of Canada through the Canada Book Fund and from the Province of British Columbia through the BC Arts Council and the Book Publishing Tax Credit.

LIBRARY AND ARCHIVES CANADA CATALOGUING IN PUBLICATION

Gaston, Bill, 1953-, author
    A mariner's guide to self sabotage : stories / Bill Gaston.

Issued in print and electronic formats.
ISBN 978-1-77162-171-7 (softcover).--ISBN 978-1-77162-172-4 (HTML)

    I. Title.

PS8563.A76M36 2017   C813'.54   C2017-902694-1
                                                               C2017-902695-X

For Vaughn, storyteller

9	Levitation
29	Carla's Dead Wife
51	Kiint
85	Anonymous
103	Hello:
121	Oscar Peterson's Warm Brown Bench
141	The Church of Manna, Revelator
165	The Return of Count Flatula
185	Critic
205	Drilling a Hole in Your Boat
223	Acknowledgements

LEVITATION

THE SUNDECK WAS CROWDED TOO BUT BETT FOUND A corner just vacated by the caterer's appetizer cart, maybe due to those looming charcoal clouds. The young woman pushing the heavy cart, saying *beep-beep* as people grabbed up shrimp and mini samosas, had a noble prettiness about her, a fine Roman nose, and would have been the age of Bett's daughter had she ever had one. Catering would be a perfect daughter's summer job—wealthy parties, disguised in uniform, serving intellectual inferiors. Because hers would have been a smart daughter. This was really good wine she was gulping, the smooth stuff you weren't supposed to gulp. Two more things to pin on Brian—an eternal lack of a daughter, and this gulping of wine.

It was a retirement party for one of Brian's bosses, at the home of the biggest boss, the one who answered only to Japan. Brian didn't like Bett using "boss"; tonight she would use it happily. This party might almost have been fun if Brian hadn't blasted her sideways. Had she been blasted out here to the deck or had she escaped? Maybe it was the same. In any case, she felt better out here in the air.

The party was a costumed affair, especially the women and their pastel sweaters with three-quarter sleeves, old-school blouses and pointed boobs. Apparently a *Mad Men* theme. Brian hadn't told her. Not that she would have cobbled up a costume anyway, and he knew this—but he hadn't told her, he hadn't bothered. She was already out here furious with him, and now another reason. Though she felt less furious than confused. This felt more serious than anger. She really should be alone to think, but on cue her shoulder was gently elbowed and now she watched her fingers remember how to pinch up a proffered joint. This was hilarious. To have a bygone toke here, of all places at her husband's corporate party, furious, surrounded by nylon stockings and neon plastic purses. Men in ties on a Saturday. Costume ties, but ties. But this joint, she must be out here with the younger crowd. No—she pulled in just enough smoke for it maybe to do something—these were middle-aged people, like her. The young corporate-skinnies were inside sucking up to the bosses. She'd seen one young thing, butch-haired in a black pencil skirt, place a spread-fingered hand on the wrist of a stubby old fart and exclaim, "Oh, Mr. Lister!" *Oh Mr. Lister?* What was this place! She was glad to be out on the deck with the middle people who weren't trying so hard.

She looked down at her dress, deciding to love it. It was raw tobacco silk, billowy. The pattern was tiny ochre elephants and ostriches and possibly gourds that you had to bend in close to see. The effect was retro-hippie, which would make her the guru trendsetter for all these fifties sheep. She'd heard that *Mad Men* was sort of about that. Friends had insisted she watch it if only for the fashion.

A bearded guy smiled at her and she realized she'd been snorting.

"What?" he asked.

"Who is 'Mr. Lister'?"

"The comptroller." He maintained the smile, giving her nothing, expecting nothing. "You're, um, Brian's partner, am I right?"

"What does he comptrol?" She knew the term, it was like an accountant.

"Everything." He inexpertly took the travelling joint, kept it well away from his face and passed it along. She wanted more, but he didn't offer it.

"I think he's about to get laid."

"Really!" The beardo wasn't sure if she might be serious. He wouldn't like it if she was and he wouldn't like it if she wasn't.

"I think he's about to take his comptroller out."

"Now what a horrible thought." Smile steady, he edged past her and away.

Maybe she should put the brakes on. Or maybe she should take her foot off altogether. She was on her third or fourth fast glass because Brian had insulted her in public. In front of his co-workers. She found herself with feet oddly apart, breathing shallowly. Was it the joint doing this? She could tell it was stronger than way back when. Brian had insulted her in his jokey way before, she'd lived years of it, but tonight was different. It felt like a last straw.

Another smiling young man professionally approached her, demanding to know who she was. He seemed okay, his glasses were humble and his skinny tie was black on black with embossed skulls, risqué given the environment.

"Yup, *that* Brian. Cullen. I'm all his."

"We like Brian," he said, in a playfully qualified way. This young fellow's name was also Brian.

"You do?" Bett did a funny nausea face.

He asked what she did and Bett was glad for the assumption that she did something. She ran through it—substitute art teacher, custom tile artist and hobbyist painter who had sold seven paintings in her life.

"Seven and counting."

"You're a starving artist!" said young Brian. He said he was also in the arts, web design.

Web design. Bett tried for a spider-and-fly web quip but arrived at nothing not clunky.

Normally she would've liked this party. The retiring boss was someone named Suzie, apparently a vice president, Purchasing. In the living room she was getting a musical farewell. Someone had made a playlist of the songs that were number one on the charts at milestones of her life. A fifties doo-wop ditty marked her birth, first grade was a Ricky Nelson, "Age of Aquarius" played a bit later and so on. A new VP, Ted Warren, who Bett knew from a barbeque Brian once hosted at their place, stood to introduce each song, saying, "Okay, picture Suzie all dressed up, going to the prom with the biker her dad didn't know about," and amid laughter the song would start and Suzie, sitting in the armchair of honour, blushed and laughed and squirmed at yet another corny iconic tune, as if she had been responsible for it. Bett was born in the late seventies but knew even the earliest songs, like "Yummy Yummy Yummy I Got Love in My Tummy," which Bett suspected had not been a number one at all and that Ted Warren was having fun with the retiree, who happened to be his outgoing boss. Bett watched Suzie being a good sport in her chair. She was letting her hair go grey in streaks. Trying age as an accessory, almost succeeding.

Earlier in the party Bett was inside listening to these milestone songs when Brian had insulted her. "Aquarius" played and their pack—Bett, Brian, Cindy, Doug and some others—began talking about astrology and ESP and the birth of yoga and so on, and Bett went off in search of a bathroom. On her return Brian spotted her and yelled across the room for her to please grab him a Heineken. She spun round and penetrated the crowd at the bar and eventually got him his beer, and even a napkin. She made her way back, nudged his elbow and handed it over. He took the bottle without looking at her and without thanks. Standing at attention, he raised the beer to show it to everyone.

"And *that* is how it's done. Levitation. Thank you." Brian bowed.

There was mock applause and smirking. Doug announced that it was his turn and he would now magically irritate the neighbourhood. He slid his hand into his pocket, dug around a bit and, outside, an SUV began its rhythmic howling.

Perhaps because of the expression on Bett's face, Cindy leaned in with an eye-roll to tell her they'd been talking about telekinesis and that *everyone* admitted to at some time trying to move stuff with their *mind*, how silly, and *Brian* said he actually knew how to do it, how to make a beer come to him without moving a *muscle*.

"So, good joke," Cindy said awkwardly, hooking her thumb at Brian. Bett was aware of still having no expression on her face. She looked over at Brian rocking on his heels at another punchline, jerking his torso as if in laughter, mouth closed. She considered his thick black hair and how he'd had to shave a second time this afternoon before coming to the party, deep in his body that dark rooty urgency that refused to quit.

It would have been okay if it *was* a joke and not a corny piece of shit. Or if, after his corny piece of shit, he had included her in some way. A complicit smile. A twinkle in the eye. She was a prop in his stage show and got stuffed back in the box.

He did eventually bend to her to murmur something, about himself. He informed her, "I haven't told that one in ten years."

And he meant exactly ten years. You could do nothing but believe him when he said such a thing. Brian's memory would qualify for one of those "mn" words. He was always surprising her. Last week, for instance, while eating dinner, braised lamb shank with potatoes, he paused to regard his forkful of peas.

"Remember your cousin's wedding in England, Alice and Tony's, when we went south for that weekend? And in that restaurant in Dorset, we were having lunch, and there was that cold soup, cold pea soup with mint, and we both loved it, but you loved it more. You said it was like eating life itself. You said it was the combo of peas and the mint. But that's what you said. 'Life itself.'"

This wedding was a dozen years ago. Closer to fifteen. She couldn't even remember the year. Did she remember Dorset? A little. Lunch? No. Cold pea soup? Not at all. She didn't remember spooning up and tasting life itself.

Brian remembered more about her past than she did, especially details. At first she felt flattered by this kind of attention, this apparent unflagging interest in everything she did. When he told her things about herself, she listened with an uncomfortable trust. It was embarrassing to be told that her pantyhose had always run on the left side, or that actually she *had* tasted tripe. She came to feel like she lived in a vast room, the walls ever shifting and indeterminate, with Brian watching her from his shadowy corner, taking notes. Recording every stumble. Last week he insisted that, years ago, she offended a bystander while doing a funny Bengali accent. He insisted it was Bengali.

Out here on the deck she felt not so altered, post-joint. Except the sky seemed way broader. And the sunset had been trying to seduce her, that tangerine streak having unsuccessful sex with those dusky mauve clouds, but still wanting her to watch. She turned to accept some wine being poured by another wandering caterer's helper, not her noble daughter but shorter and with a silver nose ring. She wasn't meeting eyes and had the air of barely tolerating these older, costumed fools. Suddenly what had to be the hostess barged up and insisted to the caterer's assistant that Bett wanted a clean glass for that. Bett and the girl had been happily watching the nice new wine gurgle into the half inch of old, and were apparently both guilty of outrageous unsophistication. It wasn't like they were pouring red into white, making pink.

"That's ridiculous," said the boss-wife. "Don't let her drink that. I'm getting her a new glass." This she said spinning away, back toward the kitchen.

"And a bucket and a straw," Bett called after her, mostly for the server's benefit. Bett hoped the boss-hostess didn't return. Though it was hard being hostess. They were crazy by definition. She couldn't tell if the woman's yellow dress and helmet hair was a costume or not.

Bett turned for the caterer girl but she had already moved along to cheekily try the identical faux pas on none other than the bearded guy who, hearing what had transpired, had a palm over his glass. She wandered off with the air of uncertain employment status and a shoulder chip. Though this second daughter was less knowable, Bett felt a kinship.

Bett drank her wine with wakeful haste, making sure to taste and thank its glory. How could two good wines be worse than one? She wondered if another joint might happen by. She hadn't had this urge in years, or maybe ever. Turning to an attractive commotion in the deck's farthest corner, which was banked by a density of flowering bushes, she heard "Look at the *sweet*hearts!" and "Are they robins?" She made her way over and peered between the shoulders of a bowling champ and either a hooker or prom queen.

A sizable nest sat in a main crotch of branches. Another newcomer asked if there were eggs in it and the bowler said, "Watch."

With a fingernail he scritched a branch near the nest and three open-beaked bird heads rose, quavering as if in a breeze, pleading with weak cheeps. Which must come from their throats, Bett determined, because the mouths stayed straining wide. Covered with thick lids, their bulbous eyes hadn't opened yet. Even featherless they had the coloration of robins. They quavered in that breeze, life's testing breeze, which was just their own straining.

"Dumb as flowers," Bett said.

"They're *so cute*," the prom queen admonished.

"There's a *nest*?" This from the scrunch-faced hostess, who was upon them. She said the word like they'd found a nest of rats, or traitors, hiding against her house. She carried Bett's fresh new glass aimed upside down.

As she leaned in at the birds Bett hurried away, back to her corner of the deck, desperately not wanting to negotiate that clean glass. Emerging now from the house was the host and big-boss himself, Mr. Ward, Robert Ward, wearing the most bemused of looks. He held well out in front of him another joint, as yet unlit. It looked machine-made. He spoke to whomever might listen, knowing everyone would.

"Here's one. It must be the last one." He turned it in his hand like an enigmatic puzzle. "I didn't know people would actually be smoking these." He tried to hand it off but all were shy. "Don't worry," he said, and lurched in a silent fake chuckle. "I'm not taking down names."

So the weed had been a nostalgia prop all along, procured like Suzie's playlist and the two lava lamps in the living room. When had weed become such an innocent thing? Bett stepped forward and took it from him. Mr. Ward stood planted, smiling at her. He looked eager to watch.

Another woman who didn't care, wearing an awful plaid skirt and boxy white blouse, approached Bett pointing a propane barbeque lighter while making a noise like a jet plane. Her costume was hideous, and then Bett noticed the two turquoise barrettes and understood she was ugly on purpose. They got the thing lit and Bett took a long draw, then handed it away and off it went. Robert Ward smiled broadly, on the verge of applauding.

"You don't smoke," hissed Brian from behind her left ear.

Bett's answer was to exhale the smoke extra loudly.

"Why are you smoking pot?"

An inscrutable dragon, she enunciated carefully as more smoke curled out, "Why do you care?"

"This is my work."

"This is a party."

"You know what I mean."

"This is a *pot* party, Brian." She still hadn't turned around to look at him. "Mr. Lister has *lost* comptrol."

"You haven't smoked it once the entire time we've been together."

"How do you know?"

"Not once. Never. Why now?"

"You should be thankful I can still pull a rabbit out of this old hat." Bett mimed yanking something from the depths of her, up through her mouth.

When she turned, Brian had already got himself away.

She squeezed back into the kitchen and the wine lineup, planning on two glasses of their finest. The oldies tunes were into another loop, but without Ted Warren's funny announcements, and "Age of Aquarius" was ramping up again. Bett marvelled as its idealism unfurled, the lyrics a fountain of naïve splendour. "Mystic crystal revelation," my God, what? "Harmony and understanding," yes, ISIS is somewhere laughing their hoods off at the dawning of that.

One glass was empty by the time she'd explored a long hall, traversed a bedroom and found the ensuite bathroom she'd been directed to. Only after she finished and emerged did she take in the grand bedroom. It was larger than her living room. Fainting couch, fireplace. A stand with ornate water jug and basin for a vestal virgin's ablutions. On the walls, original art. She recognized none of the artists, which was rare. A little depressing. There was just so much brilliance out there, young brilliance skyrocketing past her. She found her depression depressing.

Sliding doors opened onto an ensuite sundeck and she heard the laughter and voices of another party underway out there. When she walked into and flattened her nose on the screen door's mesh she spilled not a drop. No one saw. Humming "Age of Aquarius" to herself she daintily slid the screen aside and stepped through, caught a heel on the track, again spilled nothing, then turned and daintied the door closed behind her, still humming.

The master bedroom's deck was another marvel. Half-enormous itself, it lent a view of what was pretty much a bona-fide forest, one that separated this suburban estate from the next one along. Here was the kind of elegant seclusion only the most elite bossiness could bring. At the deck's far end, two suited madmen lounged ironically in padded loungers with a half-dozen others standing alongside, elbows cocked with drinks. So here is where the white-robed boss-hostess perched of a morning, plotting her day, eyeing any possible nests out there.

Bett saw the bratty private partiers intent at something, craning forward. Then, *whoa*, they lurched in unison as something whirred past. Their focus was a beautiful hanging hummingbird feeder, an oversized cloisonné marvel. The glass was grey crystal and a subtle rainbow of enamelled hues gathered and appeared to melt into the red base. The partiers were absorbed in the hummer action, oohing and ahhing the rufouses, or that would be rufi, so Bett announced, "Hummingbirds are roofies for hippies." But no one heard, or at least no one laughed, and then there was a brief hummingbird fight, one dive-bombing another. The victor hovered at the base of the feeder, guarding its sugar-water from the partiers. It actually appeared to expand its tiny chest before zithering off.

Bett said, "That was no fight, that was a quickie," ashamed because now she was trying too hard, but they liked that one. Two women followed up with jibes about their husbands' invisibly quick foreplay, and one of the loungers good-naturedly groaned "guilty" and hid his face in his hands.

Hummingbird sex, that would be good to see. Incandescent little bang. Union of candy. It would make a good meme. Poster art. Nature's naughty sugar.

At the edge of the circle of brats, Bett heard herself proclaim, "I got shit on once by a hummingbird." When no one budged she repeated it and several people turned to smile quizzically. So she told them, jamming together the details, how at a resort while sunbathing poolside under a hanging bank of feeders, the red plastic ones, the hummers were ubiquitous and soon ignored, and then on the second day a bird buzzed above and she felt the tiniest thread of cool wet anoint her left breast. A wee tinkle of frozen silver. In a second the poop was gone, eaten by air. Brian hadn't quite believed her. He had smiled knowingly.

"I was lying on one of those," is how Bett summed it up for them, pointing at the lounger, "and a roofie," she tapped where the silver had tickled her, "*shit* on my *tit*." She hated that word. She hated both those words.

Brian's voice boomed behind her.

"That's *good*, that's *good*! I knew a guy who did this experiment with hummingbirds—" Brian was talking as fast as she'd ever heard him, "—and he built this hat ringed with feeders, like those beer-can-holder hats and you drink from straws—right, like that"—he pointed to the fellow making a sucking lummox face—"and he sat real still and hummingbirds came, and they got used to him and his hat, so next he taped the red plastic feeder flowers right over his ears, and the hummingbirds actually shot their little tongues in, *right to his eardrums, and it tickled like hell and he said it actually began to hurt!*"

Bett had already edged out past her husband as people said wow and whatnot. He needed a shave again already, the black rootiness so plain on his face.

"Bullshit," she said, aimed at him alone as she slid the screen door open and stepped through. He'd never told her that story and it was a story he would tell. Or maybe he had told her. Maybe he'd told her that story right after she told him hers, just like now.

Back in the palatial bedroom she stood at the foot of the bed, a bed so vast it made the strewn coats and purses look like children's coats and purses. These were people's real coats and real purses, not their costume ones. Surprising that at a place and a party like this, coats were still flung onto a master bed. Bett could hear the music loop, the retirement tunes. She pictured old Suzie in there squirming and politely pink. God, good for her, she had climbed the ranks with these people, she was even Brian's boss—so please, Suzie, don't retire, don't quit, but why did your name have to be Suzie?

An ironic English droner sang that he was too sexy for his shirt, a wonderful song, Bett had forgotten this one entirely. She needed the bathroom again, but probably no more wine. Now the guy realized that he was too sexy for his love, and Bett thought it the best line she'd heard in ages, maybe ever, in fact it was a mystic crystal revelation it was so right for times so out of joint.

She was leaning on the bathroom door frame and Brian had her elbow now. "Why are you doing this?"

Breathing? Listening? "Good question."

He hesitated. He squeezed her elbow harder. "I feel abandoned."

"Oh Jesus."

"I do, Bett."

"*You* cut the cord. *You* did it."

"What cord?"

She didn't know what cord. She didn't know it was there until it was cut.

"Leave me."

Bett tensed to hear her omission of the "alone," wondering if he heard it too.

"Remember," he said, talking fast again, "before we got married, one time you thought I was ignoring you at a party, you felt abandoned, it was Pete and Joanne's, and later on we agreed that, at any party, or anywhere at all, with other people around, even if we weren't in the same room, we'd be together. 'Holding invisible hands,' you said. Always."

He regarded her, his head tilted, waiting. She said nothing. She faced away from him. He took her shoulders in his hands and drew her back to his chest. When he spoke, his chin softly bopped the top of her head.

"Always *with* each other. 'Co-conspirators,' you said."

"That wasn't me."

"Yes it was."

He gently tugged her shoulders rhythmically, one then the other, so there was the suggestion of a figure eight. It was maybe something she'd once liked.

"I remember now," Bett said. "It was someone else."

She left her husband's hold and flung herself to the middle of the hosts' bed. It was a bed so big you could do some hands-and-knees exploring, which she did. One of the private-party madmen was making his way past the foot of the bed toward the bathroom, wincing and tiptoeing as though she were not to be disturbed. At the bed's very centre she flipped onto her back, atop the scarves and purses and prudent raincoats. She saw that

Brian hadn't left but regarded her patiently. From his shadowy corner. He would think incorrectly and to his peril that she was doing any of this because of him. She began a snow angel there on the fashionable and expensive textures and colours, enjoying the mix of friction amongst the fabrics, texture being just as good as colour for its range. Her husband's odious texture was part of it. She realized that when doing a snow angel you are trying to dig in, you are trying to fly down.

CARLA'S DEAD WIFE

MY FAMILY—THAT IS, MY THREE SISTERS—ARE ALL OVER the map. Carla thinks she's wise, June actually might be wise and Bean's stayed country and is wise without knowing it. I'm the brother and they generally forgive me that, plus I'm granted a modest superpower because I'm oldest. Most of us like to drink, which can grease the family tectonic plates. I'll blame what happened between me and Carla on this, on three or four lunchtime beer. I had a long-held secret to share. I was just trying to be nice.

It was Thanksgiving but a special one, trumpeted for months to gather family living away from Broadbend. They know I'm a loner and keep a rough house but it was my turn, and I agreed to do my part to nurse along what might be our last family tradition. I felt doubly obliged, squatting as I do in the old family place, alone with five bedrooms. It's all I can afford, being underemployed. It wasn't smart to pursue a landscaping career in a part of the world where everyone's neighbour owns a backhoe and the planting of trees for other than a windbreak is seen as affectation.

WE HAD THE THANKSGIVING EVE PARTY FIRST AND AS ALWAYS it was the rowdy one, making for a subdued Thanksgiving proper, a good thing if only because it means the food is nicely cooked and we might get through a turkey dinner without wine elbowed into our laps. I wanted to tell Carla the first night and get it over with.

But the entire Eve party Carla sat pregnant and wide-legged in a chair holding court. Becca, her new partner, stood on guard behind her, sometimes massaging Carla's shoulders but otherwise staying mostly quiet. Carla kept up a stream of information, requested or not. Though the youngest, she has always been a lecturer who, again, thinks herself wise. She's forty now and I'm forty-nine, and even when I was nineteen and she was ten she'd inform me about this or that obvious thing. I never had a problem with her being gay, in fact I mostly admired her for it, especially how she never wavered or apologized, despite coming of age in a small town. Kind of the opposite, in fact. Even her lesbianism, if that's what you call it, she had a way of displaying, like she had the key to life and we didn't, and now just watch her walk down the street arm in arm with it.

I popped into the kitchen from time to time, intending to finally tell her the truth about Jacinthe, her late wife, though it was soon obvious that I had to get her alone. The kitchen was crowded like kitchens always are but now even more so because of the formality-ham I'd been commanded to cook—well, heat up and slice into fingerlings—along with the rum-raisin dipping sauce that no less than two sisters sent me the identical recipe for. So people were shoulder to shoulder, dipping ham. And there was no end of people surrounding Carla with questions about her baby-to-be, and she was all ready with the too-much-information. I'm no prude, but since straight couples keep the sperm-and-eggy details to themselves, perhaps gay couples could do similar, especially given that their details can tip into the spectacular. Which is maybe why they get hauled out at parties, fair enough. Lesbian pregnancy can indeed be colourful, especially when the weird-donor stories come to light. And as it turned out, had I been in the kitchen hearing a few more of exactly those details, I probably would have stayed shut up, despite the secret that had burned me for years. So to speak.

That night we were all distracted anyway by what was going to happen to Iris's husband, Philip. Iris is June's daughter and one of my several nieces here for the weekend. None of us had met this Philip before. He looked maybe thirty, and someone said a professor of something. An "itinerant scholar" according to Iris, which I think meant eternal grad student who couldn't land a job. So he had my sympathies. But he wasn't likeable, sitting there in my living room, perched on my best chair in discomfort. When someone isn't comfortable in your house you don't like them for it, it's automatic.

Philip had his hands clasped between his knees, leaning forward, listening hard at the music I had on. None of my music is social, and the playlist of old Eno was about as close to toe-tapping as I could find. It was good enough early-in-the-night music, until someone, probably one of the nephews, would come in disgusted and swearing and stick their own pod in my dock with something rowdy. But this particular Eno was a cool, patient homage to Pachelbel's *Canon*. Imagine that tune slowed in molasses, beckoning from an even darker depth.

"I don't—I don't *know* about this," declared Philip, out of the blue and too loud into what had been a long, respectful period of us just listening. "It's—*Canon* is one of the—I mean yes it's been accused of '*melody*,' but—Can you just *take* it and use it? Just walk into a studio and—" Bug-eyed, he dialled some knobs in the air. "—and just, contribute *nothing* but some ambient, you know, *breezes*—?"

Half of me registered his words and the other half the specific people in the room. My niece Iris smiled fixedly, also aware of two of her uncles standing in cowboy boots and watching her husband with a slight lifting of the eyelids that indicated redneck glee. They were a couple of bored sharks who'd swum in to find a lamb paddling around the shallows. They were checking on the size of his arms, his neck, guarding the family gene pool even if they didn't know that's what they were doing. My family can be cruel to anyone not fitting the pack. If they picked on Iris's husband, I could already hear his hissing outrage loading up Iris, who would then walk it into the kitchen and spread it back into the family. If bad feeling could be tracked with dye, it'd be a real study to sit back on a family couch and watch the indigo shade one room and then another. I'd already heard a *Why aren't you being nice to Iris's husband?*, which was likely why Dwayne and Pete were out here in the first place, fists full of my ham and staring at Philip. Maybe they'd "be nice," or maybe things would go dark blue.

My pod was on shuffle and "Baby's on Fire" began, followed by every face in the room wincing, even Philip, though probably for different reasons. I admit I was a bit surprised that not a single relative of mine found humour in the music, its nasal Brit snippiness. Eventually Philip took a loud breath and sat back, publicly disowning the song.

"Don't like it?" challenged Dwayne. The rest of us paid attention.

"It's—it's—"

"It's fucked up?"

"*No* it's just that it's—it's just too obvious. Like it's—"

"It's obvious?"

"Yeah it's—"

"Well fuck me."

"*Baby's* too *big*. It's the first thing you'd think of."

"*That's* fucked." Dwayne still hadn't blinked or taken his eyes off Philip.

"He should have said, you know, *niece* is on fire." He turned his face up to Dwayne. "Or, *uncle's* on fire."

"Way better," Dwayne said.

Only now did I see that Philip was drunk. I wondered if he knew that Dwayne here was his wife's uncle, which would make Philip a death-defying ironist.

In any case, the party lurched this way and that and things went dark or light from room to room. I drank too much and lost track while keeping busy with food and spills and arranging taxis to the hotel. In the flux I missed Pete and Dwayne and my sister Bean dragging Philip downtown. There were upstairs beds to set up, and teenagers to direct to cots I'd borrowed. Stored blankets and pillows always conjure for me the word "family," and in some ways define it.

•

MY DREAMS THAT NIGHT WERE BENT IN THE WAY THAT bends the morning too, and I woke to yelling from outside my room. It took some time for me to hear it for what it was, my sister June getting yelled at by her daughter Iris, the husbanded niece. I tried not to listen but through the thickness of my pillow I gleaned that last night her Philip failed to return, his escorts coming back empty-handed. I recalled that Bean had had on one of her moody T-shirts, the *Pick and Irradiate*.

I found it easy to picture a sweaty Philip struggling in some cop's bear hug—the cops here aren't all that bad if you're white and don't take serious swings at them. I can remember one saying to me, through my blur, "*Once* more, Robbie," not unlike a strict mother. I was awake now and peeled back the pillow, blinking through the grit. Nothing more from the hallway; Iris had retreated. I was worried not so much about Philip but for today's party, the actual Thanksgiving. I pictured my turkey thawing in the fridge, an organic one as commanded from afar.

In the kitchen, over my ham omelets came news that sections of his body, drawn and quartered by pickup trucks, could be claimed at—I was fantasizing that as the real Philip stumbled in. Ignoring our hellos he spun and peered out the kitchen window as the cop car rolled away. I saw the cop lift a hand, but Philip did not wave back. I was about to judge him for this when I recognized that particular nakedness of face and understood that he usually wore glasses but wasn't now, so he'd seen no wave.

"Philip. Omelet?" I asked.

He turned my way with red slits of disbelief just as Iris flew into the kitchen and grabbed him. He continued to watch me like I was one of my brothers-in-law and he was compiling what to say. Iris dragged him to the living room and got his hissed story, and I thought I heard him cry but I could be wrong. Iris charged upstairs to launch into a couple of brothers-in-law already into their post-omelet naps. A reluctant posse was formed to go find Philip's glasses.

"You say they're black?" Dwayne asked over his shoulder on his way out.

"Black."

"Do they have any other features? Springy arms or anything?"

"*They're black fucking glasses*," Philip shouted face down on the couch, Iris rubbing his back. "*In some skuzzy fucking bar.*"

Iris added in loud monotone, "Don't bother coming back without them."

I gathered from the day's snippets of rumour that Dwayne and Pete had indeed turned on him and he staggered off and was blindly trying to find his way back here but ended up in a parked bus on the grounds of the Deaf School. He couldn't say how or why he'd gone into the bus. I have knowledge of such things and my guess is he drunkenly knew that a bus would have a padded bench, for snoozing. Shaken awake, he was disturbed that the cops had pointed questions concerning exactly why it was he'd been found in a vehicle used to convey children.

In any case, I didn't have my talk with Carla the first night, though I don't know why I'd expected anything different. Today was traditionally the more sober one, and Carla and I would connect.

We used to be close. We used to sit pressing shoulders on a crowded TV couch and we both liked it, I could tell. We still were close, I felt, so much so that we'd never had to say a word about it. I never trust the bond of friends who go on about what good friends they are, or those couples who make displays of a second wedding ceremony. I think the mark of a bond is that it never gets mentioned. Though most likely it's thoughts like these that make my relatives whisper, "Okay that's another reason he never got married."

Carla and Becca descended to the kitchen as I hunkered over the breakfast dishes and they proceeded to organize a private brunch. As they picked through my cupboards asking if there was quinoa or tamarind and so on I couldn't tell if I was witnessing the pregnant or the foodie version of fussy. I enjoyed their surprise whenever I had what they needed, and I confess liking that Becca's hipster haircut was now a bad Rod Stewart after her good night's sleep on it. When city-girl Becca asked if the eggs were vegetarian-fed and I shrugged and answered free range and she nodded, I almost gave her the news update that free range are never vegetarian-fed unless you count ants, grubs, spiders, centipedes and rodent scat as vegetables.

Carla gathered and instructed, then sat wide-kneed on last night's chair to watch Becca cook. These two were notable for their shared lack of hangover. Save for Becca's punched hair they looked alert and on-game. Without seeming to spy, I checked out my sister's face. For the last ten years—Jesus, it was more like twenty—if we were lucky Carla and I saw each other maybe once a year, ever since Jacinthe dragged her off to the bigger and better. Despite the plumminess of her current condition her face had been squaring into a semblance of our father's. As had mine, so people said. Yet Carla remained the prettiest of my sisters. She had been a match for the stunning Jacinthe herself. I couldn't help but compare them both now to Becca, whose features were kindly but round and plain, and looked plainer still in proximity to my sister. It would be like a fox mating with a volleyball. Carla's eyes were black and piercing, her nose perfect, her lips a fleshy lure. The word "handsome" sprang to mind, a word I sensed I could no longer use, even in jest, not anymore, not like in the early days of her disclosure when I'd call her "little brother" and she'd laugh and hook thumbs in her belt loops and stick her pelvis out. Even when Jacinthe first crept from her dalliance with me to a serious one with her, Carla tolerated it that one time I joked, "At least it's between brothers." But I could see how politics had changed her vocabulary over time. It wasn't just our father's face I was seeing in her but a deep wariness that also looked tired. When you lose your humour, you lose more than just your humour.

I finished the dishes. Again I poked at the turkey, gigantic there on the rack I'd cleared for it mid-fridge. I'd had my doubts it was going to thaw in time but my finger was now leaving a dent. Carla asked me from her chair how I was doing, really, erasing the empty pleasantries we'd exchanged thus far. Though Becca was here with us I told her how late middle age was maybe bringing with it a calmness. Becca harrumphed about my "late" middle age, but I explained the math of being a single year from fifty and guaranteed not to see a hundred. I've never liked "middle age" as a euphemism, any more than "golden age" and how it pretends we'll all be grinning in glowing syrup at the end. The bloom was burned off my rose two decades ago, and I'm not scared to admit it.

Speaking of hangovers, my guilty sister Bean came down mumbling that both Philip and Iris were demanding some soup and making her get it, and somehow blaming her for some shit, and so where was some soup. She knew full well that turkey soup day was tomorrow, when broth from the night previous soothed all survivors. That and a long, muted football game, though none of us were what you'd call fans.

All I had for her were two individual-size cans of soup, a mushroom and a beef barley, for which Bean exhaled her thanks. I caught her considering pouring both in the same pot but stopped her with an arm and found her a second pot.

Becca laughed at all this and Carla looked away impatiently. Last night people had given their friendly condolences about her not being allowed to drink and how she must be looking forward to that first beer, and Carla smiled and nodded, not caring to tell them she hadn't had a drink in years. I understood I might be the only one who has paid attention, through all the years and parties, to Carla not drinking. Jacinthe didn't drink and Carla had followed suit. Or taken orders.

While her soups began to bubble, Bean had her head in the fridge overlong, maybe cooling it down.

"What's with—*Hey.*" She sounded almost scared. "*What's— the drumsticks.*"

Finally someone had noticed. I bought the biggest organic turkey they had but it didn't look like enough, so instead of buying a second I bought four extra drumsticks, which weren't organic, but who's to know, and I stuffed them artfully into the plastic turkey bag, two per side, achieving a bulbous centipede effect. Until this morning it had been covered with egg cartons and a leaning box of wine.

"I was going to cook it and carve it that way too," I said. "Whaddya think?"

"Go for it," said Bean. Then to Carla, "You see Robbie's funny turkey?"

"We did," said Carla.

This kind of thing would've been funnier back when there were smaller children zooming around, sure.

Bean left with two soup bowls filled to the brim and held high on a tray, the three of us wincing and listening hard as she climbed the stairs, expecting the worst. Despite Becca's protestations I finished their new dirty dishes.

Carla sat doing the daily crossword she used to do years ago, and Becca drank tea. I realized they were keeping me company. I wondered how much Carla and Becca had discussed Jacinthe, and decided that of course they'd discussed her to death, so to speak. Jacinthe had died two years ago now, and Carla got together with Becca not long after. I heard they'd become good friends during Jacinthe's decline. So maybe I could share my story with Becca as well. In fact maybe it was the proper thing to do. And, really, when I thought about it now, it was a story with a happy ending. The upshot being how glad I was that Carla had ended up with someone good, Becca, and had escaped spending her life with someone bad, Jacinthe.

"Carla," I said, finally. I cleared my throat. I had had my second or third beer and I felt good and clear.

My sister was looking at me, eyebrows up, ready to smile. She held her belly in gentle hands.

"I wanted to talk with you about something, actually tell you something—Tell you *both* something, which is mostly that I'm really happy you two are together."

"Robbie!" said Becca. "That's really sweet."

My sister just smiled at me. I recognized some love in those eyes, but mostly some wait-and-see, which might have goaded me.

"And, hey, congratulations." I twisted the top off my third or fourth beer and tilted it at Carla's swelling.

Becca said, "Well thank you again."

"But, anyway, Carla, and I guess Becca, I wanted to tell you how happy I am that you're with Becca and not, you know, not with Jacinthe. I mean and—" I saw an identical half-lidded caution overtake both of them, and my bad sentence stumbled even further. "It's not like I'm glad about *why* she's no longer on the scene. I mean, hey!" I smiled wide and shook my head but they weren't helping me out. "It's just that, there's this thing I never … No, maybe I just shouldn't say anything, Carla, sorry."

"Okay, Robbie. You didn't like her. Fair enough. And apology accepted." Her eyes had me. No trace of a smile. "But do say more."

"Hey, forget it. I have a turkey to make. And a beer to drink." I tipped the bottle upside down and joke-glugged it. Still no mirth from either of them.

Carla said, "No, tell me something about my dead wife."

Face blank, Becca watched her as one does a rising thermometer.

"Okay, I will, but this is not about dissing Jacinthe. It's about how happy I am that you two—" I pointed my beer neck at them both in turn, "—are together."

"Understood." My sister's hand flew up to her shoulder where it found and quickly squeezed Becca's.

"So really it's just great, and I'm just happy that it's *you* two having this baby together."

Carla's face stepped back into unreadable. Becca, on the other hand, leaned herself out of Carla's seeing range, made wide, wide eyes for me and sliced her hand quickly back and forth across her throat.

•

I SAW IT THREE TIMES. THE FIRST TIME I DIDN'T UNDERSTAND what I was seeing, and the third time I was watching for it. Each time was at the Regis Hotel, where anyone who wasn't a redneck went to drink. It's gone, of course, but it was the homely place I met Jacinthe, who was as lithe and exotic as her name. In fact, during introductions across the table I'd already had a few and when I heard her name and mumbled, "Onomatopoeia," and nothing else, it may have sounded like the slimiest pickup line but I think it was actually my ticket in. Shy smart people attracted her. She never could understand why anyone was shy. It was something out of her range.

In any case Jacinthe was a smoker, an elegant and mindful one, plus she didn't drink, so the main point is that she was never sloppy with her cigarette. The first time I saw it, I hadn't met her yet. What happened was, a few tables away a guy suddenly shouted, "*Ow! Jesus!*" and leapt to his feet. He'd been burned on the forearm by the cigarette of the woman to his left, who had long hair and whose face I couldn't see. The woman didn't get up and was oddly unanimated in her apology. The guy, who kept grabbing his arm and wincing, looked angry and suspicious.

The second time made me remember that first time and remember it with icy alarm, because the second time it was me. We'd been going out—that is, having sex after another night in the bar—for exactly a month. I was in love, I was helplessly in love. Jacinthe laughed away my wanting to go on official dates, just the two of us at a restaurant, for instance, or a weekend away. The two times she did give in, once to a movie and once to an over-the-top pheasant dinner at Benducci's on her birthday, she seemed bored. Even angry. We both knew I was trying to claim her. She wanted a social scene, where she wouldn't abide even the appearance of being claimed. For instance at the bar we wouldn't even sit together, and all evening I'd show her how long I could go without staring at her, the whole time waiting for her little look that signalled my life was about to turn perfect because now we were going to my place again, to bed.

What is it about sex like that? You become a hungry baby. A brainless puddle of want. I can't say much about Jacinthe and me, except for bad poetry. Poetry for the deluded soul, so it can blindly masturbate again. But I have my theories. I think that one of her problems was the sex itself. I think it made her open up and lose control and get skinless like the rest of us, unable to speak or look you in the eye. She hated that. She hated me, anyway. She hated me so much for seeing her bleed that she had to fucking cauterize the wound.

We weren't even sitting side by side the night she burned me. She sneaked over and sat while I was talking to my buddy Larry, that is, Law, across the table, about DDT and eggshells. Law's "Who *needs* birds?" got me going, which was all he was trying for, because Law liked a wild bird as much as anybody. Then a searing pain had me on my feet. In retrospect, I sounded exactly like that first guy. And like with that first guy, Jacinthe wasn't overly sorry. She only half looked at me and said something along the lines of, "My mistake, let's move on." That night we didn't go home together. I pretended it was because I was mad at her, but we both knew. It felt like her physical turning away from me. Our romance, if that's what it was, ended raggedly and silently over the next few excruciating days.

When it happened a couple weeks later I was alert to it, which was a miracle in itself because of my moping drunkenness. So I wasn't exactly watching, but when I heard another yelp like that—a burn does elicit a telltale reaction—I located the table, way across the room, knowing I would see Jacinthe in the thick of it. The victim was a woman this time, a bit older than everyone, paunchy and wearing glasses and a dress shirt, a local government type. She had a fucking hole in the sleeve of that pale blue shirt.

I also discovered around this time that Jacinthe had been going home with my little sister, who had recently turned twenty-one and occasionally graced the Regis. She had been out of the closet for years—again, there hadn't been a closet. She was smart but not at all shy. Also in retrospect, I'd say that the fact it was my sister with Jacinthe eased my pain a bit. How weird is sex? My agony was somewhat pacified because Jacinthe was still making love to a member of my immediate family. It was a confusing time.

A few months later Carla moved east, and later I learned it was to join Jacinthe. Then the years began their sighing past, and there came news of the wedding, my invitation to which was joking and half-hearted, and it seemed not so many years after that came the rumours of the breast cancer, and during all that time Carla's face became the biggest welcome surprise at any Thanksgiving or Christmas. Jacinthe never did come back to Broadbend, and I never did tell my sister what I saw her do.

•

CARLA HAD SENSED BECCA TRYING TO SILENCE ME WITH the throat signal and she reached up again to find Becca's hand.

"Okay Robbie, tell me all about her."

"I should of told you a long time ago but—"

"And by the way that was her real name."

"Well, so you've said." I still doubted it. "But, come on—"

"I can't believe you're still trying to get her."

Entering the kitchen with the tray of soupy bowls, Bean asked, "Why wasn't it her real name?"

In a drab voice meant to stay outside of the main event, Becca said, "It was her real name."

"So why was it a question, then?"

Which was for me but I ignored her. We all ignored her when she announced, "Now Iris and June aren't talking to me." And no one watched her open the fridge and peer in again, though I did wonder for a moment if these several spats within my family provided the right stage on which to present my many-legged turkey.

"Carla? I don't want this to become a thing."

"Too late."

I'd anticipated and pictured this very moment, though apparently not clearly enough. But I was very happy the third burned person had been a woman. If all three had been men it might have looked like I was accusing Jacinthe of being a man-hater, which wasn't what I thought at all. The world was full of man-haters, the lesbian world maybe even more so, and many women had reason to hate, maybe even to burn. I didn't want Carla to think I didn't know this. I wanted her to know that Jacinthe was an unbiased sociopath.

"Okay, well." I decided to man up and tell her. Bean was still here, finding solace in the fridge, but sometimes the more family that's in on it, the merrier.

I lifted my forearm and angled it at Carla. I'm pale and the circle is brown enough to be seen across a room. "This has a story to it."

Carla's lack of curiosity was unnerving. Becca looked away. Then she closed her eyes, a second looking away.

It's funny, that is, strange, how often things dawn just that one second too late. Suddenly I knew why it was that, when I first brought all this up, Carla had begun stroking and palming her swollen middle. As if to soothe the unborn child who might be listening. And I just that second made sense of certain exclamations issuing from last night's kitchen, ones like "I didn't *know* you could freeze the eggs!" and "So you froze some when you heard? Well what a lovely thing." Now I knew whose eggs, and who Carla had been trying to soothe with her hands.

Feeling hollow, I brought down my arm. There are times when the truth should not be told.

Becca still had her eyes closed, and my sister was undoing the button at her wrist. The room went bright as she brought her forearm up, and my God there it was. But darker, fresher. I'd guess about two years old. Carla's hand was in a fist. Her delay was perfect and now rose the middle finger. This, mixed with the gently wise smile, was confusing in a way that will have no end to it.

KIINT

IF ARNIE WAS HONEST WITH HIMSELF HE WOULD ADMIT the fish farm job had saved his life and had probably kept on saving it. Toba Inlet was an ocean dead end with no road in, no power, nothing. At night or in the sudden middle of a day it could get so quiet you could stand there—just stand there—and hear your heart beat.

It was just guys. Women need not apply. Arnie didn't know how they got away with that, these days, but no women, and no alcohol allowed. Almost like it was designed by someone with his best interests in mind.

The one link to the outside was a VHF radio, good only to call nearby boats or the company office thirty-nine miles by water in Campbell River, a one-room piece of shit across the road from the government dock. Arnie could still picture it from the day he was hired, that edgy guy at his metal desk, blaming him when some government papers didn't match up with what was on his stupid screen.

Some days were more isolated than others, no water taxis, no feed barged in, no fry barged out. Arnie called them Robinson Crusoe days, after one of his favourites. At low tide he'd walk the shore, out of hearing range of the bunkhouse, the guys yelling their video game deaths. Away from gulls swarming the mort bins like junkies on a spilled bag. Away from the thump of the buried generator, the camp's beating gasoline heart. He'd walk until he could see and hear nothing but what had always been here. Toba was a mountain valley filled with ocean, dramatic if the clouds lifted and you could actually see above the trees, the mountains' rock shoulders and snow way up top. But even the cloud was natural, and a big part of the isolation. Socked in, was the expression. He'd stand on a barnacled rock, sometimes hearing his heart, still mostly glad he'd left the city, the bad kaleidoscope of people. It was easier here. At his feet, a simple current kept seaweed flattened to a rock. A stone's throw out, the sleek black dome of a seal's head. Then he'd be bored and walk back. He always had a book going, and industrial headphones for the bunkhouse noise.

The only real work happened by itself, in the salmon pens, under water. Arnie swore he could feel the fish down there, barely finning as they digested their food and swelled heavier with milt or eggs. Doing their job. They had no eyelids, and it was funny thinking of them down there big eyed in the darkness.

That was camp, and that was his life, until Kiint came to wreck things.

HE ARRIVED IN THE DRIZZLE OF LATE MAY, A NEWBIE STEP-
ping off the water taxi with two other guys back from their days
off. He was medium height and thin. "Nondescript" would be the
word. From the way he didn't pause on the dock to gaze up at
his new home you could tell he knew this country. It wasn't just
Arnie watching from the bunkhouse; only nine guys lived here
at any one time and a new face in camp was news. Soon he'd be
shoving food into his face across from you. Five feet from your
head his nostril might whistle all night. You might get to know
the smell of his towel.

He ate a prepackaged sandwich alone at the corner table,
and they let him because he could have come to them. From
his efficient chewing and the way he gazed at something far off
but definite, Arnie saw he was different. Who knows why but he
thought of a fox waiting in a den of mice. "Sated," for now.

When the guy finished and sat sipping coffee, Arnie wandered
over. Arnie was both the biggest and the oldest here, forty-five
to their twenty-five, which is maybe why he did the Walmart
greeter thing. Or maybe he still wanted to think loneliness was
a simple fix. The newbie's hair was oily and he looked tired. He
was on the frail side for general labour, resembling more the
pencil-neck university type who dipped test tubes in the pens
or syringed juice from a salmon. But he was dressed in shit so
general labour he must be. Arnie could swear guys wore the

dirtiest crap on purpose, as if to show how hard they worked. If these camp guys paused at a downtown corner, people would drop change at their feet.

He shook Arnie's hand limply, but Arnie knew that meant nothing. When he said his odd name it brought to mind another guy here, a First Nations fellow who introduced himself as "B. Paul," leading to confusion he never cared to correct:

"Bee *Pall*?"

"Pleased to meet you."

"That's an odd name."

"No it's not."

Quizzical looks gained nothing and only later would you learn his name was Bob. Arnie didn't know if Bob found dignity using an initial or if he was just pissing off another white guy. He'd always been alert to names, because growing up a Bacon wasn't fun. He always wanted people to think of the actor Kevin, or even Sir Francis, who might have been Shakespeare, but everyone just thought of bacon, and in his school years he answered to Pig. When by some huge fluke he was the first in his crowd to get laid, for a while he was happy being called Makin'.

Introducing himself, the new guy had a faint accent, maybe German. Arnie predicted to himself the jokes that would be made about him being a Norwegian spy. Every operation along the coast was Norwegian-owned, so all new guys were of course Norwegian company spies.

The spy said his name was "Sint." Arnie saw that he wasn't drinking coffee. The tea bag was red, and you could smell its herbal sourness.

"'Sint'?"

"Yes."

"That's it?"

"That's it." Now he looked up. "Like Madonna."

Arnie asked him to spell it and he did.

"No way. A *K*?"

"That's right." He was falsely smiling now.

"But can a *K* be, you know, an *S*?"

"The two *I*s do it." He held Arnie's gaze. His eyes were the light blue that feels too active. He was barely willing to be liked. "That kind of hard," Kiint said, "can't take that much soft."

Arnie waited a bit, but that was that and it was his turn. He got Kiint to smile for real at "Arnold Bacon." He said his folks were from the old country and couldn't have known what names might be hilarious in a new one.

Kiint asked, "Do you think you ended up here because of your hilarious name?"

Here meant two grey buildings in a clearing hacked into the trees thirty-nine miles by boat from a WiFi signal, flush toilet or woman. For basically minimum wage. It was a job any guy could get. Arnie snorted at the question but wondered if it was 5 percent true. It didn't bug him that Kiint might be right. It

KIINT 55

bugged him that this newbie thought he could know, in one minute, something about him that he didn't know himself. He was about to say, You probably *chose* your Eurofag name so fuck off and die—but he took a breath instead, an infantile temper being one of the actual reasons he was here.

A finger tapped his shoulder. It was Clarke, the super.

"Arnie? Since you're already sort of doing it, show him around."

It was a bit of a rebuke since he should have been outside brushing down E- pen ten minutes ago. Clarke told Kiint to come by his office when they were done. The office was a closet where timesheets were kept, but Clarke liked saying "my office." It wasn't easy being bossed by a guy twenty years younger than you.

In the mudroom they donned rain gear. Kiint shrugged off the offer of a spare floppy hat in favour of his own weird little cap, and as they walked past the land tanks and out the ramp to the first floating pen the wind hit and Arnie could see him pretend not to feel the cold drips down his back. The rain came so hard Arnie had to shout the age and size of the stock. Shouting that there were females topping a hundred pounds over there in D-pen, he was surprised to feel his pride. Shoulders up and stiffly listening, Kiint had no reaction to any of it.

Then they stood in the nice quiet of the feedhouse with the various pellet bins along all four walls. It smelled like ripe pet food and gave off a red dust that was hard to breathe. Centring the room was a computer station covered with plastic sheeting, which Arnie grabbed up to flap like a bedsheet and get the dust off. He'd heard it was red dye to turn their flesh salmon coloured, which made sense. He watched Kiint take it all in.

Arnie took him through all the programs. He was mostly just avoiding work, but guys liked to hear about stuff. It was impressive gear. They had the new compressed air system where a computer key chose what food to blow down what pipe to what pen, where a carousel sprayer, like a robot spinning to feed a thousand pigeons at once, showered the water with pellets until the fish lost interest. Too much feed would sink through the fish and out the pen and be lost, like dimes through your fingers. Kiint stood patiently while Arnie scrolled through the codes that troubleshot clogs and spills. Arnie joked about salmon gluttons that fought their way up the dry pipes to gorge here in the bins, and Kiint either wasn't listening or didn't find it funny.

"Wanna see the morts?" You could smell the mort bins from anywhere. Morts were dead salmon and they were knee-deep in them even here at a brood farm. At the market farms it was way more. Guys pretended the deformities were entertaining—fish with shoulders, or plaguey bumps, "buboes" was the word, which B. Paul called boobs. Some fish were skinny, little more than swimming spines that somehow stayed sort of alive. You didn't go out of your way to look at them. And it was nice to know they were working on that stuff, looking for answers. Fish farms really could maybe someday feed the world.

Before Kiint could answer, they jumped to the roar of a shotgun, not twenty feet from the door. It was because one of them was a newbie. Ha ha.

"That would be MacLeod," Arnie said. "He just fed a crow to the crabs." His heart was still going. "A headless crow." He looked out the window, but couldn't see MacLeod. "Or crowless head."

"Scared me," Kiint admitted. Rocking faintly, he gazed into neutral territory.

The fact was, guys killed birds. Next to video games it was the main fun. But only the noisy ones, the crows and gulls. A shotgun got used rarely because it made gulls disappear and not dribble back for a week. Guys got expert at slingshots. He once saw guys have a go with a paintball gun, hitting only the odd bird but screaming like little kids when they did, the gull flopping there, splotched yellow or blue. He saw guys invent da Vinci-like machines, and even for a non-birdkiller it was cool to watch an innocent-looking net fly down as hidden weights released, taking to the sea floor twenty gulls stupid enough to swarm a pile of morts magically served up to them.

Kiint didn't want to see the mort bins. He put his cap back on like they were done here, and fair enough, they pretty much were. Arnie reset the computer and yanked the plastic sheet back over.

"You have any questions about anything?"

Kiint looked around as if for a piece of gear he hadn't understood. "No."

It was strange that Kiint didn't ask a single question about the place. Not one. Newbies loved hearing about stuff. The predator cage, steel mesh that kept seals, whales, otters and sharks away from the soft-mesh pens, and how some, seals mostly, got stuck and drowned trying to get through. Or the bubble curtain that kept toxic plankton out. Or how algae and fish shit clogged the mesh so fast that each pen needed oxygen diffusers bubbling away down there at all times or the fish would suffocate. A fish farm was like a giant dirty aquarium.

"So this your first farm, or—?"

"Bella Bella."

"Didn't that one shut down because of the—?"

"They cleaned it up, they said. Now it's expanding."

"Really." The politics of aquaculture were beyond him.

Before leaving, Arnie opened the antibiotics closet to show him the arsenal and Kiint didn't even look—in fact he thought he saw him shudder. Arnie understood how, for some people, even fish disease might feel like their own.

Back in the rain, slogging up to the bunkhouse, Arnie was moved to shout a last fact, one Kiint probably knew.

"So this is one of five brood sites on the west coast of North America. All the salmon, for all other farms, for restaurants, groceries, everything—it starts right here."

Kiint said, "Cool."

Arnie wanted to yell that here was better than the market sites. All that butchering, all those morts. Humping all that bad meat to the bins, to be barged away under a spiky bonnet of screaming birds and dumped who knows where. Here there was less of that. Here it was all eggs and milt and helping a million silver darters grow.

Arnie did yell, "It's okay here."

At the bunkhouse door they smelled weed. Arnie turned.

"You know it's a dry camp, right?" He tried to say it in a non-revealing way. When the time was right Arnie might tell him he sought out dry camps for a reason.

"Yes."

"So everyone compensates by being high all the time. Everyone except me." He added, "Especially weekends." It was hilarious that even out here and in a job with no weekends they still used weekends as an excuse. They had a giant carved octopus hookah they called Mr. Saturday Night.

He showed Kiint the showers and DVD players and whatnot, and now Kiint was smiling sideways at him because, sure, anyone with a brain could figure out this stuff for themselves and, sure, he was taking work-avoidance too far. But he still found it strange that Kiint didn't have a single question about the place. Simple ones like, Does it always rain like this here? Or, How do you claim fridge territory or dib the stove? Or, especially, This is grizz country, right?

Kiint did pause to scan the books stacked in three towers beside Arnie's bed. Except for Bob Paul, who tackled an occasional thriller, he was the only one who read. And he was proud of it, though no one gave him reason to be. If anything they found it uppity. Kiint's eyes caught on several titles but Arnie couldn't tell which. His taste was eclectic and his aim was to educate himself. He saw he'd left in plain view his notebook for jotting his new words, and if Kiint bent to touch it he would get his hand stomped.

But Kiint wasn't curious and still had no questions. Now Clarke was in Arnie's face and hooked his thumb at the general outdoors, wordlessly ordering him back to work, wise enough to smile as he did so.

Kiint said an obligatory thank you and met Arnie's eyes for the second time that day. It felt like an icy insult. Kiint didn't exactly look through him. He saw him as part of the problem.

·

ARNIE HAD NO REAL SUSPICIONS UNTIL LABOUR DAY ITSELF, when Kiint went into action. Maybe he did have suspicions, but they were of the vaguest kind. One was Kiint's early request to stay on-site and work the Labour Day weekend, which besides Christmas was the one time the place all but shut down, only a barest skeleton crew staying on to make sure the stock got fed. When Arnie heard of Kiint's request, his eyebrows went up; it was the kind of request he made himself. Some people like to avoid holidays and go into hiding. In any case, it would be just him and Kiint working Labour Day.

There was also the way Kiint wouldn't talk about fish farms. He just wouldn't. Later it was funny for Arnie to recall telling Kiint the nasty secret that their salmon might be iffy, and that in fact one grocery chain was going to stop selling it, and Kiint, eyebrows up, saying, "Really?" And the time Kiint said, "Yikes," when Arnie told him he'd read somewhere about mercury in the feed.

There were other small clues. As when Kiint came back from his first days off with a wet suit, and the next time a scuba tank, but then never used any of it. Also the lack of an air compressor was stupid, because it would limit Kiint to a single dive. But Arnie figured Kiint wasn't getting around to it in the same way the rest of them weren't getting around to trap prawns or invent bird machines and ended up smoking weed and playing vids instead. Arnie would glance up from his book and watch them slumped there, bodies rigid only in the arms, faces an ugly blend of tense and dead, stabbing and jerking their controllers like what was left of their zombie lives depended on it. It made him think of "Boredom is rage spread thin," from one of his quotation books. Sometimes they did go on hikes, but only after lots of "cajoling," and only in groups, shouting and singing to warn bears of their approach.

Kiint hiked by himself. He had been on-site a month when Arnie followed him. Not followed, exactly. The mountainside was impassable with underbrush and there was only one path, so he couldn't help it. Ten minutes out of camp he emerged from the dark tunnel of forest onto a mossy rock knoll and stumbled on Kiint just sitting there, cross-legged, some sort of yoga thing. Kiint looked irked to see him. Arnie said sorry and spun and turned back, which of course made it worse, and he thought he heard Kiint sigh. He felt like some sort of creeper, which is probably what he looked like. After a minute he heard, "Bacon." He stopped and turned and Kiint trotted up.

"Starting to rain," he said, short of breath, explaining himself.

"It is."

"You ever see spirit bears up here?" he asked.

"They aren't in Toba. They start next inlet up." Arnie waited. "There's grizzlies here, though."

Kiint shook his head. "No no no, they're here. I was just wondering if you've seen any." He glanced at Arnie, the brief ice of those eyes.

"Nope."

"The grizz will show up in about a month, right? At the river mouths? For the *salmon*?" Kiint snorted quietly. He might as well have said, "For the real ones," this sort of sarcasm the closest he ever got to humour.

They walked. Arnie was angry-quiet because Kiint was walking with him like he was doing some loser a favour. Arnie had his own brand of humour and he asked Kiint if he was Norwegian. Kiint smiled but probably just thought this Canadian was stupid about accents. He said he was from Holland but he had lived all over, most recently New Zealand.

And so they became friends. Or, "friends." Arnie knew it was more a case of two soloists falling warily into each other's orbit.

•

IT WASN'T LIKE THEY DIDN'T KNOW THERE WAS SOMETHING wrong with this business they were in, from days off being accosted in some bar by a health-foodie or commercial fisherman accusing them of sins against the world. Arnie used to live in these bars, he knew what yelled beer-spit looked like when it flew out a mouth a foot from your face. You know your farm spreads disease and kills wild runs? What idiot works for minimum and the profits go to Norway? Why you raising Atlantic salmon in the Pacific? Don't you know they're escaping, they're spawning wild, they're taking over?

This last one was definitely wrong and the guys knew it. If one of their fish blundered out a hole it wouldn't have a chance in the real ocean, let alone muscle miles upstream, get laid in the gravel and reproduce itself. The slobs in their pens were barely fish. If you had any doubts, troll up a fall coho and battle a twelve-pound silver bullet hard as a sprinter's thigh.

But so what? Arnie has imaginary arguments with Kiint even now. He considers writing him in jail. Fish farms might still feed the world. There were way worse jobs and way bigger sins. It was a *job*. Teachers keep teaching even though most kids don't learn a thing. The landfill is overflowing but garbage men do their rounds. Are the workers part of the problem? It's a debate worth having, Kiint. Not that he ever said an accusing word but Arnie saw that look, more than once, saying he should know better.

When Arnie first got there he actually thought he was doing something good. And he hadn't done much of that, historically. Proof of this lay mostly in what wasn't: No friends, no family. No skills he could bank on. No credit rating. He wasn't even allowed a passport. He had told Kiint enough of this to imply that he was in Toba Inlet not just because his name was Arnold Bacon.

Anyway, after, the more he thought about it, the more he thought that Kiint had been only obvious. It was strange that more guys didn't suspect him. Or maybe they did, and just didn't care. Or forgot. Or were pleasantly puzzled by whatever unfolded. Weed could do all that.

Everyone worked ten days then waited for the aluminum taxi to come and roar them through waves and rain to five days of real life in Campbell River. The boat's arrival back was a spectator sport because guys climbing out told a story. Knowing he was watched from the bunkhouse, a guy might grab his crotch and hunch, feigning the rawness from epic screwing. Or mime a fatal headache, the epic drinking. Arnie saw guys wave bulbous bags of weed, hump the new porno vids in their backpacks, wield a Canucks-signed hockey stick and fake slapshots out to sea, or wave a chub of venison pepperoni they intended to auction. Mostly it was that: meat. They'd hoist heavy coolers onto the dock, give a thumbs-up to say they filled the orders for chops and steaks and burger.

Except for Kiint. Unloading his cloth bags of salad and quinoa and whatever, he might flash a salute to their equally ironic hoots. He wasn't liked. Which was fine by him. They ignored him and he ignored them back. The point is, he was a card-carrying vegetarian. More than that, he was vegan—what sort of vegan worked for minimum at a meat farm? A *tainted* meat farm?

His oddities seem glaring now. He just didn't belong. He was a visitor from a wider world. He knew things no one else did. Things about this place. Things about them.

On one of their hikes together Arnie learned something about what Kiint knew. From the start they had wordlessly agreed to walk in silence, with only functional talking—Was that a marten? You sure that's a morel? This walk had begun in sunshine, now it began to pour, and Arnie had had enough.

He stomped and shouted in rhythm with his feet, "Fuck, fuck, fuck, *rain*."

"No!" Kiint said. He stopped and he grabbed Arnie's shoulder. Eyes crinkled up in pleasure, Kiint yelled, "It's *rain*forest!" He laughed shaking his head, like they were in the Arctic and Arnie had just complained about the snow.

"I guess."

"No! It's a *treasure!*" He put his head back, arms out like Jesus on the cross, and let the rain fall into his eyes.

As they walked on, Kiint described where it was they were. He was "sanctimonious" but Arnie let him vent. Pointing at the mud on the path he said they were at the southernmost edge of the largest temperate rainforest left on the planet. Almost chanting, he detailed how much it rained, why it rained, how that tied in with ocean currents, how it all might change and how the change might be gradual or "silent-spring sudden." There was still hope if governments were made to work together. It all came flying out as if under pressure. He described how the rain—*this* rain, he said, and he rolled his face under it to make sure every inch was anointed—created the ice pack, which fed the rivers, which bore the tiny salmon out to sea. He spoke of a tightly knit drama. At one point he shrieked a single note of incredulous joy, describing something Arnie thought he'd heard before, which was that the sheer quantity of salmon dragged off by bears and eagles and wolves had over millennia fertilized the trees hundreds of metres up either side of the riverbanks, and today salmon was in the trees' DNA.

A minute after he'd finished talking and Arnie had said nothing to fill the gap, Kiint said, "I'm sorry."

"That's okay." He was stunned to hear a silent man talk in paragraphs.

"I love this place," Kiint added, unnecessarily.

This love might have been enough reason for this guy to be here, but Arnie sensed there was more.

In the bunkhouse, keeping mum, Kiint had managed to become a piece of furniture. He'd been on-site two months and it was another month till Labour Day. One evening a young guy, Kenny, was frying up some salmon he'd scooped from B-pen. It was verboten to steal stock, but if guys were too spaced out to get their meat order together, there it was swimming right outside the door. Clarke wouldn't do anything, since one salmon was so much less than a drop in the bucket.

As it sizzled, poking and worrying it non-stop with the spatula, Kenny asked no one in particular, "So when's this shit safe?"

He meant when were the antibiotics flushed out. The med-feed had ceased in B-pen months ago, and a few guys mumbled that it was okay. Bobby Paul joked that Kenny should go ahead and eat it and cure the gonorrhea he probably had.

This kind of talk was always floating around. So who knows why, but that night Kiint, quietly munching on his bowl of roots and fronds, lost it. He dropped his fork on the table. His hand hovered over it, his eyes closed.

"It's never *okay*."

No one said anything. Kiint didn't deserve a response. They were going to let it pass but Kiint wasn't. He actually smacked the table with his palm. You could hear the spice of his accent climb into the rest of what he said.

"The antibiotics are gone, Kenny." He waved his arm in the direction of the water. "The antibiotics are now in the crabs and shrimp and sea urchins. What's still in your piece of shit is mercury, lead and dioxins. The Ruhr valley is in your piece of shit." Shaking his head, he grabbed his fork and stabbed his greens. "Enjoy, Kenny."

It was Clarke who laughed, and then sang, "Whaaaat?"

Others were laughing too and Bobby Paul asked Kenny if he knew there was a valley in his dinner. Kiint ate quicker, wanting to get out of there. Clarke waved an arm at the same water and in the same way Kiint had, mocking him, and proclaimed there was no way any of that crap was in the air up here in Toba Inlet.

Kiint put down his fork down gently. "Where does the feed come from?" he asked.

"The big blue barge?" said Bobby Paul, who hadn't stopped grinning.

Kiint said it came from Norway. Aquaco bought it from themselves so they didn't have to pay taxes on it, but our country being stupid was beside the point, the point was that the feed was from North Sea plankton and fish waste that had absorbed "the airborne hell of industrial Europe." In a gesture as theatrical as it was bizarre, Kiint pointed at Kenny's sizzling fish and listed off Mercedes-Benz, IKEA, Volkswagen (saying the W like a V) and ten other companies no one had heard of. A guy playing video games yelled at Kiint to go back to fucking Norway if he didn't like it here, and Clarke shouted back that it was Norway Kiint appeared to be mad at.

Clarke added, "Well what the fuck." He seemed to think that, as boss, it was his job to win this argument, if that's what this was.

"No one's making you work here, right?"

Kiint appeared to come to his senses. "No," he said quickly. "I'm sorry." Then, "Eat your fish. It's good fish."

Emboldened, pulling on his coat, Clarke added, "Keep it to yourself for fuck sake. This place is bad enough without *your* shit in the air." He made a show of almost slamming the door. Being the boss, he pretended he didn't smoke weed by always going outside to smoke it.

Kiint wolfed his bowl. He looked angry, but Arnie wondered if he didn't also look afraid. Arnie was waiting but Kiint didn't look his way. If he had, he might have seen that Arnie knew something was up. There was just no way a guy like him was here by accident.

•

IN THE REMAINING WEEKS LEADING UP TO LABOUR DAY Kiint kept his distance from Arnie, other than a few silent walks, and even then it seemed he was being careful not to show how much he loved the inlet, or the rainforest. When he returned the two Farley Mowat books he'd borrowed he wouldn't even say if he liked them or not when Arnie asked. Arnie had to admit that he was a little hurt to be lumped in with the rest of them. It was difficult to admit to wisdom in a man so much younger, but Arnie did. Kiint hinted at a vaster, more intelligent world, one that Arnie had apparently let slip by. Something he saw in Kiint made him regret the puniness of what he'd chosen for himself. So it hurt to be shut out like that.

On what turned out to be their last walk, a week before Labour Day, when they stopped at the apex of Bald Head Rock and finished catching their breath and taking in the vista, Arnie was angry at the silence, angry at being shut out. One thing about fish farm life was that he didn't get angry much, so when he did, it was easy to see it. And now he was angry that he was angry.

"Why are you doing this?" he asked. It sounded corny, like something a lover would say, so he hated himself now too and was about to stomp back down the trail.

Kiint turned to face him. Arnie sensed he was being read. But Kiint must have read him wrong because he answered a different question than the one Arnie asked.

"It's just a job. Right, Bacon?"

"Right," Arnie said, not knowing what he was agreeing to.

•

THE FRIDAY OF LABOUR DAY WEEKEND, AT LOW TIDE ARNIE trudged the rocks to his Robinson Crusoe spot. It had been a year since he'd bothered coming out here. He stood and breathed. He held his breath and tried to hear his heart. Then didn't care if he heard his heart or not. He was surprised by his restlessness. He couldn't settle. Maybe it was the looming fall. Fall was when you started school again, and hockey. It was the time to stop screwing around, stop partying, time to get in shape, start projects. Arnie could feel the outside world beyond these mountains—big and busy, rumbling, buzzing, working, and though he hadn't forgotten that it was mostly bullshit, there was something out there he was missing. His life was easily half over and he had to admit he'd blown this half, first with trouble and then with hiding. He wasn't sure how but it was Kiint who had prodded him, who had lit this fire. Kiint who had checked him out and decided he wasn't worthy, lying here reading stupid books.

He scanned Toba Inlet. Its water, mountains and muffled sky were so familiar that he could be standing anywhere. He unzipped and pissed into the calm water at his feet. A slow and ignorant current moved the foam to the left. A crab the size of his thumbnail crawled back under its rock. Arnie laughed at himself, more sad than angry. No good book was pulling him back to the bunkhouse. For whatever reason, he didn't like fiction anymore. And he understood he'd been restless for years.

And that afternoon, not a minute after the water taxi picked up the crew and disappeared around the point, Kiint destroyed the camp radio with a hammer. This was so nobody—that is, Arnie—could call for help, or whoever it was you called when the guy you were stuck with in camp had begun methodically smashing the equipment to pieces and burning everything else to the ground. Arnie liked to think Kiint did the radio first not because he thought Arnie would call, but because he knew Arnie would get into trouble for not calling. Arnie still wasn't sure if he would have called or not.

·

THE FOLLOWING WEEK, IN WHATEVER NEWSPAPERS HE could buy in Campbell River, Arnie read all he could about it and he learned Kiint's real name. All five brood sites on the Pacific coast were attacked that Labour Day Friday. One of the five "eco-terrorists," Andres Vandover, hailed from Amsterdam, so that had to be him. One was a New Zealander and another an actual Norwegian, which Arnie found funny because that made him a kind of double agent, and you could only imagine the weird ironies he'd endured, the bunkhouse jokes about Norwegian spies. The other two were women, a Canadian and a Brazilian, and how they got hired on he could only guess. They were at the sites farther north and maybe they were more progressive up there.

There was mention of a "manifesto" that authorities weren't making public, in the spirit of not negotiating with terrorists. Nor did the authorities reveal much else, since court cases were pending, and the news stories were littered with the word "alleged." The attacks were coordinated, but why terrorists would target fish farms was still a mystery. So ignorant and unclear were the stories that Arnie wanted to call and tell them that the only reason to attack just brood sites was to destroy how the salmon farm industry replenished itself. There was no other reason—it was appalling that they couldn't decide on even that much. Also, they said his site was located in Toba Strait, there being no such place. There were comma errors too, and more than one wrong "it's." Journalism had really gone downhill, and it was all the more obvious when you knew some of the truth of things yourself.

The reports said damage to the Toba site was the most severe. So Kiint had done the best job. The New Zealander had managed only some computer system damage, "Fish mortality was minimal," and he got badly beaten up by the skeleton crew. (Arnie tried to picture the guys jumping on Kiint, and it was easy.) The other three sites were badly damaged but would "in all likelihood be made operational again." Toba could not.

In the manner of today's media they were dubbed the Fish Farm Five, another piss off, because somehow it cheapened what they did, and tried to cheapen the regard Arnie had for Kiint, for Andres Vandover, though Arnie wouldn't let it.

It had been truly amazing to watch this young guy work so hard, and nothing selfish about it. Because whatever Kiint believed—was he protecting the environment? Protecting the world from bad food? Chipping away at capitalism?—it was for others that he did it. This is what Arnie couldn't get over. In the outside world there were people like this. Sometimes they found their way up Toba Inlet.

Watching Kiint hustling to finish the job before they came and put a boot on his neck and took him away, Arnie wondered what Kiint's damn hurry was, he had all weekend. But unlike Kiint he didn't know about the other four attacks underway or that they would be putting two and two together soon and sending in the troops. As it turned out the cop boat didn't arrive up Toba until dawn. Followed by the coast guard—Arnie was surprised those guys were allowed to carry guns—and then, he couldn't believe his eyes at the overkill, a hovercraft. It was when they were putting the cuffs on Kiint that Arnie rethought the selflessness business. He was standing well away, in the first line of trees, pretending to be afraid, going with Kiint's advice to avoid resembling a friend. But the look in Kiint's eyes, amazing. He didn't know what to call it. It wasn't selfless. Kiint was just absolutely proud and loving everything he'd done, he was loving the cuffs, he loved that cop's shove, and he was loving it all so much that it had to, it just had to be selfish. It was a feeling Arnie recognized and wanted. He had no word for it yet.

•

HE HAD RUN TO THE NOISE OF KIINT SMASHING THE RADIO, and hammer in hand, Kiint came striding out the bunkhouse door, saw Arnie coming and flashed a palm.

"Bacon, stay out of my way."

Kiint broke into a trot up the path to the generator hut, bouncing the hammer, testing its weight for a job bigger than the radio.

Arnie stayed out of his way. But he was thrilled and he had to move so he got himself away from there, and once up the trail and into the trees he couldn't hear anything from camp. It took only a half hour to get up to Bald Head Rock and when he reached the clearing, breathing so hard he brought his hand to his heart, he stood agape at the mushroom of black and brown smoke tumbling up from where he'd come. In this vista of giant things—mountains, ocean, sky—the smoke was a new creature that held its own. Arnie stayed up there as long as he could stand it. He wasn't scared of Kiint at all. Something spectacular was going on and he was missing it. He set off back, finding it hard not to run, enjoying the luxury and speed of the downhill stride. He did wonder if there'd be anywhere to sleep tonight.

He didn't know why he chose "Waltzing Matilda" but he broke into song when he emerged from the woods, not wanting to surprise him. But Kiint wasn't there and Arnie felt foolish and hoped he wasn't being watched from the woods. The feedhouse and generator shack were off the peak of their flames and were two collapsed heaps of hissing orange embers and metal, heat mirage throbbing over them. A grand old cedar next to the feedhouse was scorched halfway up its length. The feed bins were still releasing an odd smoke, the hint of black suggesting the gear oil poured in to help things out.

Arnie yelled, "Hey *Kiint*. What's *up*?"

Nobody answered, and Arnie could hear the silence behind the embers' hissing. It was that intense calm of aftermath, that stillness of a morning house that had been violated in the night. Kiint's absence was a presence.

He would tell Kiint to get over it, he was going to help. Or watch. Arnie didn't know what he wanted. But he was a lot bigger than Kiint, if it came to that. Arnie was still happy with this most basic of laws.

The sun was behind the mountain now and in the blue dim he walked past the land tanks and, in their thousands, all the tiny fish were belly up. The pump was dead but they wouldn't have suffocated this quickly—he must have thrown some kind of poison in. Who knows what else Kiint packed in those bags of salad? The odd light helped make it stranger still, the tiny luminous pearl bellies forming an unbroken floating layer, a carpet of identical glowing shapes. "Tessellated."

He ventured out on the ramp to the pens, flanked on either side by still, deep water. Maybe Kiint had made a run for it. Maybe he'd stashed a kayak and supplies somewhere, though how he'd done that in this fishbowl was anybody's guess.

He walked the ramp to its limit, to D-pen, where the big ones were. With the bubble curtain off it was more quiet than ever, so quiet he stood still and tried to hear his heart. He couldn't. He thought he could feel the monsters under his feet, down deep, the hundred-plus pounders. On the east coast they used to grow that big in the wild and he'd seen grainy black-and-whites of rich Americans on guided trips standing beside their tail-hung trophies. As big as the ones below his feet. He stood over the black water, feeling the unseen gliding shapes, swollen with eggs and milt, bursting with so much future life. It was almost fall and they were ripening with the one thing they existed for.

Certain he could feel the immense parents gliding beneath him, something was off. He could feel it. They were badly alive. It tipped his guts. It was like seeing a turd on your mother's head. It was like a warm worm turning in your ear. Dumb giants bumping into each other down there. The giants had been brought here, from a foreign ocean, so we could grow and eat their sick babies.

The bubble curtain was off but he could hear a faint bubbling. Then he saw it, a green light, deep underwater, moving slowly. There was a moment when it might have been a sea monster, a demon, and then he knew it was an underwater lamp he hadn't seen Kiint unload. And there, scuba bubbles breaking the surface out along the rim of D-pen, slowly burbling his way.

He laughed, he hooted, he stomped his boot then caught himself. Kiint must be down there taking care of the oxygenators, so they couldn't be repaired. He had really thought things through.

That light, that little green light far below. It was like a quiet, tiny invasion from another planet, it was brilliant unlike anything else around here.

•

THE BUNKHOUSE HAD BEEN LEFT INTACT. ARNIE WENT IN and stood in the middle of it, in the coolness in front of the blank TV, and it all felt new and different. He couldn't stand still. There was no longer electricity but he knew of a propane camp stove out back. It was unlikely that any of the guys would be returning now but he felt the thrill of theft as he helped himself to their food. He unwrapped the rest of Clarke's venison jerky and gnawed on it as he worked. He primed the camp stove, lit it and fried up two burger patties, one of them Kiint's nutblend kind, which didn't smell half-bad as it cooked, and he built up two Mexiburgers, being mindful of melting no cheese on Kiint's. He toasted the buns on the blue propane flame, then plated them up surrounded by a decent salad. His he deposited on the table.

Arnie draped a white towel over his forearm to lighten the mood and walked Kiint's down to him, but stood off a ways to let him finish hacksawing the metal feed pipe. He was barefoot and had his wetsuit top off, but still wore the black pants. He grabbed a sledge to mangle the freed piece so it couldn't just be welded back on.

Arnie called his name from twenty feet away. Kiint turned bug-eyed, exhausted, head hanging forward off his neck. He gave Arnie a good stare before nodding that, yes, he wanted the food.

He took it and said only, "Don't tell them you did this." He waggled the burger.

"It's cool." Arnie unfolded the chair he'd dragged over and Kiint sat down with a gasp.

"Don't tell them we talked at all."

"Not to worry."

He wolfed his burger after first checking its contents. He smelled of extreme sweat, fish and wetsuit rubber. As he chewed he quickly surveyed the damage he'd done, and what he had yet to do.

He seemed to remember Arnie standing there.

"Bacon. You have to leave." Kiint looked at him philosophically. "It goes bad for you if they know you didn't try to stop me." He nodded with a new thought. "And they think we're friends." He stood and thrust the plate back to him, salad untouched. "Thank you, but."

Arnie hesitated taking it. When he did, he said, "Hey, I can help."

Kiint turned away, put the palm up again. "Don't joke about it."

"Who says I'm joking?" Arnie said, regretting it because it sounded whiny. And he had just understood what Kiint had said. They *think* we're friends. Kiint ignored him again, trudging off toward the ramps wagging his finger in the air, remembering something.

In the bunkhouse Arnie pulled someone's blanket over his legs and sat down to a solitary dinner, while starting Ken Kesey's *Demon Box*, apparently an unfinished novel plus other stuff he didn't publish before he died. The blanket smelled harshly of somebody's deodorant. The book wasn't that good and Arnie was bored by it. Fiction. And it was getting dark to read. He tried a flashlight for exactly five seconds before he threw *Demon Box* in one direction and the flashlight in the other, making a fantastic wobbling strobe in the room before it crashed through the window and fell out into the dark.

And then down from the ramps the clang of a hammer, the sound of which still made Arnie's heart race. He wondered where it was he should go, and if a city, what city it might be, and now Kiint's hammer sounded comical, a puny *tink tink tink* in the face of a world of steel and cement and big government. Arnie started to laugh, bouncing in his seat, mouth full of burger, ready to help take it on.

ANONYMOUS

- In ten years she'll have no muscle definition. He, too much.

- His puns. Once he called himself The Mock Less Punster and was thrilled saying it.

- He knows her complexion. You think he could put two and two together and pick a different vacation spot. Paris. Iceland.

A few minutes after her swim, already too hot, Claire lay on her stomach on the clean, raked sand, bucked once, and understood she was crying. Quiet tears, falling from her with no fanfare, almost like breath. But she was definitely crying. She was glad she faced away, and Bo hadn't seen. Because what would she say? This week was supposed to be about happiness.

Okay. Gritting her teeth against the chafing, she clambered to hands and knees, toppled onto her back, dug in her shoulder blades, took a breath and opened her chest to the sky. She groped their beach bag for her sunglasses, got them on and felt the relief of shutting out some sun. She'd give it ten minutes, by which time her front would be beyond dry, plus sprouting some new poisonous freckles. This Mexican sun was something. You really didn't want to fool with it. Its glare was serious as serious could get. It actually used to be God. Priests actually used to butcher girls here, trying to bargain with a *star*.

"You're awake," he said, lying beside her.

"*You're* awake," Claire said. He'd been snoring a minute ago.

"Hell yeah!" he said. As always, enthusiastic about the smallest stuff.

"You thought I was asleep?" She knew he heard the admonishment because he said nothing. Bo wasn't allowed to let her fall asleep and burn, that was their deal.

He flipped to his back to start his crunches. It wasn't on the list but she found it a little weird, him waking up and instantly into exercise. It was like blinking awake only to grab a half-finished crossword puzzle, or bottle of rye. What you did first thing upon opening your eyes was a kind of proof of what mattered to you. Most people wanted to check out where they were, a bit of dreamy indecision. Bo mostly wanted to be cut. But he'd never admit it to her, it wouldn't sound deep.

Beside her, he hissed and flexed. It hurt even to listen. She was beyond tired of the salt grit under her two-piece, every chafing inch of which burned; it felt on the verge of full-out bleeding.

She pictured the white fabric—always white, all her life, to give her skin at least a chance at looking tanned—blooming underneath with a blackish wine colour, like blood spreading to soak a bandage. She pictured herself on the hotel bed later, naked, a barber pole of sunburn. Bo slowly circling her, hunting the least painful spot to climb aboard. The thought of this climb made her wince, even though she suspected the contrast might be desperately good. Pierced by arrows, flayed by God, her orgasm emerging victorious. Maybe ecstasy needs a battle.

She needs her cool shower, right now, today's first of several. At home, describing what was to be their first vacation together, Bo had told her that the sand grains on the Atlantic side were small and white, while here on the Pacific side they were "big and brown and hot." He waggled his eyebrows and she realized he'd made what he thought was a decent racial joke.

It was when she realized that his humour had become a thing on her list.

Beside her, he crunched. The gripped breath, those pressurized gasps. She could so clearly picture him: perfect human wedge, toes and fingers pointed stiff at the sea. Only his bum touching the ground. Two perfect muscles cupped by warm sand. Now she could smell his armpits, plus the heated-up coconut. Those gasps were exactly the sound he made near the end of sex. She liked the gasps. But not the armpits.

This was what she'd been doing now for two weeks. When it dawned on her that they were coming to Mexico to give him a stage to pop the question, she'd panicked. Not meaning to, she began compiling a list of anything about him she didn't like. Anything that gave her pause. The panic fell to a kind of grim habit. When the list became too long, too easily, she panicked anew. Here she was now on a beautiful Mexican holiday, staring at him unblinking, her mind basically a baited trap.

    Some items were only silly, like what he called his "personality socks," pink or striped or team socks he wore to an obligatory party or meeting, socks he said freed him from "needing to say anything." But some of the list turned out to be deep gut stuff. Like his armpit smell, an angry, pungent bass note that could make her turn away. Wasn't it possibly a serious thing not to like your life partner's deepest smell? But, the thing was, she maybe *liked* the personality socks. And the same even with that smell—she would never like it but possibly she *loved* it, in that final way you might love a wolf that had you pinned and was about to kill you. Because she loved Bo. If love existed, she loved him. From the shadowy messy heap of sometimes nameless men that lay behind her, Bo had risen steady and shining, a true and sturdy comfort. She'd thought far too much about all of this. Wasn't it simple? Wasn't she making up a list because she was scared to death?

    "Can we do Old Town tonight?" she asked, purposely interrupting herself. "The Italian place?"

    She waited while he finished his set. Maybe he could think while crunching, maybe not. His face a grimace that showed his back teeth. Maybe his body was so strangled with flexing that it freed his mind to go outside all by itself and do whatever it wanted, even weigh hints from a whiny girlfriend. One who never out-and-out said so, but liked the old part of town if only because it didn't resemble the beige glitz of the hotel he'd picked.

- She will soon be a counselling psychologist. He installs computers.

- He laughs at his own little jokes. That's not what humour was built for.

- He finds her a world of mystery. She finds him sexy.

Bo flopped in the sand. Catching his breath he announced, "Food, sucks, there."

He was entirely wrong. And what he'd left out was that, in town, dinner cost money, while here at the all-inclusive it didn't. And that tonight was Blue Shrimp Night, hadn't she noticed the posters, three of them, taped up in the elevator? Nor was he repeating what he'd let slip out in the plane as it was touching down. As she open-mouth ogled the palm trees and heat haze and glowing shabbiness of Mexican life in her very first glimpse of the tropics, Bo confided in her ear that his main goal on this trip was not to get diarrhea.

He had other goals, one at least. When he surprised her with this vacation he made it sound spontaneous, a lucky fit to her spring break. But she'd watched him secretly struggling with his boss to arrange the time off. Then there was the Visa bill she found, something big from a place called Maxwells, which a Google search identified as a jewellers. And, years back, when they just met, he innocently told her he wanted to be married by thirty. He had lately turned thirty. And, she just knew.

It was now day four of six, and Bo's nervous glee had built and built. He was obviously teeing it up to do the corny thing and put a knee in the tiki-lit midnight sand. She knew his thinking precisely. She'd so far guessed correctly that he wouldn't ask her the first or second nights, because if she said no, or her lack of enthusiasm made things weird, the vacation would be awful. Last night had been a maybe, and he hadn't. So he'd do it tonight, out here on the beach at moonrise, because she'd raved about the reflected silver chalice on the water. And then they would celebrate, rush upstairs for a first time as an engaged couple, then get drunk, and have a day to recover and not have to fly in pain. That he was refusing to eat in town ostensibly because the food sucked, only cemented her suspicions. It would be tonight. She knew him this well. Which was on her list. Also on her list was that she would never not know him this well.

The food *so* didn't suck there, that's what gave him away. Two days ago, on the second day, they'd taxied in to wander Old Town, and though it was getting on dinnertime back at the hotel she hadn't wanted to leave. This waterfront had old, brightly painted fishing skiffs anchored and bobbing, often rimmed with pelicans, which she'd never seen before. The streets were noisy and smelled, and they had to dodge endless hawkers with trinkets, but it was so alive, a constant carnival. Then, Maria's. They'd walked in, lazy with heat and lured by the most seductive aroma of the day. It was packed and they were lucky to get the last table. The pizza was so good, this place would have been packed even in Calgary—the black-bubbled crust, the full-leaf basil, the high-end ham and porcinis. They ploughed in, speechless and groaning. The Mexican food was crude by comparison.

"I have a secret," Bo had announced, picking over crusts on the pizza pan. He'd ordered another margarita and sipped it looking everywhere but at her. Claire thought, this is it, and, head down, watched herself slowly tear her napkin in half.

"I'm joining Anonymous," he said.

Her look made him say, "You know, the hacking group."

She stared at him, waiting for more.

"Okay, *trying* to join. I think they're checking me out." He picked up his margarita. "Even on vacation." He sipped, tonguing in some rim salt.

"What do you mean?" She placed the two halves of her napkin on her plate.

"I'm totally joining them." He looked at her directly and shook his head as if she was arguing a point.

"Why?"

"I dunno," he said, doing an elbows-up hip hop move, thumbs and pinkies slashing around. "Fuck up da *man*."

"Who's the man?" This caught him, her taking it to a semi-serious place. She pictured him in one of those masks. No shirt on. Nice.

"I dunno, Syria." He leaned closer, tilted his forehead at her, and the light cast beautiful shadows on his cheeks and brow. "Wall Street? All the Trumps? Third World oppression? All the great stuff they do."

"How do you join a secret organization?"

He shrugged. "Well I mean *they* all joined at some point, right?"

As he launched into an explanation of something called Linux, and encryption, and the fact that they could vet him as he sat here in Mexico eating pizza, which was the "beauty" of Anonymous—he waggled his phone at her as if they were in there admiring its private contents even now—what Claire wanted to ask him was, What do you know and when did you begin to care about Third World oppression?

She interrupted him explaining an apparent contradiction between privacy and anonymity with, "Is it dangerous?"

Bo was delighted. "We're anonymous!"

He loved saying "we."

"I'm just playing around with the idea," he said, on the verge of slurring. He licked a thumb and stabbed at pan crumbs. He looked up to meet her eyes, genuinely excited. "But wouldn't it be great? To do that stuff? To actually do that stuff? Those guys are great."

"Are they all guys?"

"Well, yeah, right, touché." He bobbed his head, sheepish. "I guess you never do hear about girl hackers."

"We don't get caught."

"Well touché again." He smiled so to suggest giving up, he couldn't win. He sat back and relaxed, beyond his tequila, to meet her eyes. Telling her that of course he knew that Anonymous was the ultimate twitch game for boys. His eyes. He could always find her and meet her where she was.

"It'd be so good," he said, simply meaning it, "to do some good."

"I'm with you there." She probably wasn't. When it came to this stuff, to the human footprint stuff, she was a failure. Bo voted Green. She voted nobody. Bo often ran to work. She hadn't run anywhere since she was a child.

But it had been so clear that, two nights ago in Maria's, he was mostly just trying to impress her. And shouldn't that be okay? Shouldn't that be okay?

- She has a past, possibly a bad past.

- She likes his "hair guitar," when he stretches his hair out and strums it to a wild song, pretending to hurt himself and singing "ow" at the very best notes. But he does it for the wrong company.

- Anonymous won't want him.

OKAY SHE WAS BURNING. A TRIO OF BIG BLACK BIRDS, BO HAD called them "frigates," were slashing and diving into the surf she framed between her feet. They held an angry W shape as they hit the water and disappeared. She was beyond dry. She lifted a tentative knee, and as she did so a man came into view, a trinket hawker who, ankle-deep in a retreating wave, had paused to face her. He raised a necklace and gave it a little shake, grinning like he'd made a joke. Mostly he looked guilty and tried to make himself small—they weren't allowed within the walls. His time here was short.

She turned to watch Bo, who had just begun a set of standard sit-ups, his finishing exercise. She liked his sit-ups, he seemed relaxed doing them. Maybe because they were simple, old-school. Doing them, it seemed he could enjoy his body. He could play it and enjoy it in ways she couldn't know. He was the Greek ideal, a healthy body joining a healthy mind. And, probably, he knew himself. Maybe better than she knew herself. Bo doing his stupid, lovely sit-ups, such a boy, arcing into himself, those crazy board shorts, a carnival of sherbet colours, like they were his smile, because he was too busy to smile. But she could feel it. Bo was content here beside her, if nothing else.

His phone rang as he hissed, "*forty*." It was easiest in all ways for her just to answer it, but there was no way he'd go for that. This was almost another thing. For instance, she would love him to answer hers.

At "*forty*-seven" he unfolded himself to grab it, last ring. Breathing hard, he listened, then turned to her to say "fuckin scam" under his breath. But he lifted mischievous eyebrows and popped it on speaker, to a harsh, badly acted lecturing female voice in mid-sentence.

"—to avoid being terminated immediately. I repeat, it is imperative that you push 7 at the end of this message, and that you have your card number, address and birthdate ready. You may now proceed and push the number 7 at any time."

Bo popped the button. He glanced to make sure she was interested, then looked out to sea and cleared his throat.

"You have reached financial services," said a deep male voice with indeterminate accent. "Your card number please. State Visa or MasterCard."

"But it's, but it's ... it's American Express!" Bo's falsetto imitation of an elderly woman wasn't even close to convincing. He wasn't particularly trying.

"State the name on the card and the number please."

"But it's, but it's in the attic! I keep it in the attic! I'm sorry! Am I in trouble?"

You could almost hear the deliberation on the other end. "You are not in trouble yet. I am holding while you fetch the card. Time is of the essence."

"'Fetch'?" Bo's falsetto broke with this word. "You want me to 'fetch'? I don't know if I can 'fetch' it when it's, it's in my attic, my nasty nasty dirty attic!" Bo grabbed his mouth and turned away from the phone, convulsing. She had her hand over her mouth too, but wasn't laughing.

"If you go and bring the card and tell me the information on it, ma'am, you won't be in any trouble."

"Okay," warbled the old lady, who then became Bo. "Rot in hell you unbelievable *scum*bag."

A growl at the other end sounded almost bored and the click was inaudible.

Flopping back on the towel, Bo held his phone over his stomach, cackled and violently flexed his abs at it. The hex flex. *Yeah*, he said, flexing again. It should have been funny. At home he'd hex flex at someone from under his clothes, making a little grunt for her, it was one of their things, their good things. Maybe because she wasn't smiling for him now, he pointed himself at the trespassing necklace hawker, said, *You too buddy*, and flexed.

It wasn't that he'd done a bad thing. What could be better than wasting the con man's time. These guys destroyed old people on a daily basis. It wasn't a bad thing at all, Bo's performance. And it was funny. It's just that ... The way he said scumbag. The pinching ecstasy in his eyes. Wasn't it too easy? Could he have done it face to face? Anybody can be brave on their phone. Anybody can tweet their judgments, anybody can push angry buttons.

She winced to a kneel and stuffed her beach bag. Bo pretended to hex flex her, kicking a dead joke horse, another one of his things. She tried but couldn't laugh, could only manage a monotone, "Don't you go pointin' that at me."

He resumed his sit-ups, beginning with "*forty-eight*."

Claire watched Bo for a while. Just watched him.

Her attention was pulled away by two hotel staff, young guys in matching white shirts and black pants, striding up to get rid of the necklace hawker, who turned and grinned at their studied approach, rattling his silver chain at them, as if offering it for sale, a decent joke. Unsmiling, they each took an elbow. They could have been the man's sons.

"Heading up," Claire said. "Don't burn again."

He waited to hiss, "*hundred*," then, "'kay, see ya." Then he was an inch airborne along his whole length as he flipped onto his front. He'd be asleep in minutes, and turning a nice golden brown.

She was a few steps away, scraping big brown hot Pacific sand from the back of a thigh when he called to her, voice muffled by towel, "Just a nice little night right here, okay Claire? Bring a bottle of something out here after Blue Shrimp Night?"

She realized he didn't usually say her name. Its hope made her heart warm, and sad. She waved an okay. She found she couldn't speak. She didn't turn. She was a breath away from crying. Sobs this time. Breakage.

- He is lovely and perfect. But she has a list.

- There will never not be a list.

- Everyone on the planet has a *list*.

It was a routine they'd fallen into, Claire getting hot and heading up to shower, then nap in the AC, or maybe marvel at a Mexican sitcom, Bo doing the beach, maybe falling in with some football throwers, maybe getting a head start on the cervezas. Today, entering the hotel's cool, she tried to get angry again that her skin and its paleness unbelievably hadn't registered on him, that he'd been surprised and even hurt the first day when she didn't want to lie out there for long with him. Of course he felt like an idiot, of course he was sorry, but no one could address that, because to admit that size of mistake would ruin the beach, and ruin what was to come. She honestly hated this place. She honestly did. Even this blast of AC in the lobby felt unhealthy, and her feet rasped anew and worse with sandal sand despite wading through the stupid foot bath. And her burn lines not only hurt, they were ugly—she had pulled her bottoms down an inch and lifted her top an inch, exposing them.

- He is only kind.

- Puns are the lowest form of humour.

- A truck had delivered tonight's shrimp frozen in boxes stamped *Thailand*.

She waited at the right elevator, staring up in dumb hope at the yellow number stalled at 17. The left elevator had been "sorry temporarily out of order" their entire stay, and a fat grey strip of duct tape made as if to hold the double doors closed. A big man came up to stand beside her, breathing heavily, it seemed, merely from his walk from the beach. He joined her dumb looking up, his mouth falling open a little as he did.

"Welcome to Mexico," he said softly, presumably about the elevator situation. He sounded Texan, or one of the southern states.

"Exactly."

The number still read 17.

"I wonder what's going on up there."

He caught her assessing his stomach. This guy actually had one, and a couple of love handles. On the right wrist, a bad and fading tattoo that read RIGHT. She couldn't see if his left wrist was tattooed or not. He was casually checking her out as well. The enforced gaiety of this place allowed it, had people smiling and saying hi in hallways for no reason other than they had bought the same week of non-stop fun. She and the guy had turned almost to face each other. He was either shy or tremendously lazy. She couldn't tell. His half-smile stayed softly planted. Older by a few years. Around his shoulders, one of the room towels, which wasn't allowed. His hair was dark, black, still wet. It was doubtful he'd shaved since he'd been here. He was sort of looking at her and she at him, both expecting the obligatory joke. Claire could smell nothing coming off of him but room soap, and salt. They both looked up at the yellow 17 again.

"Somebody maybe hit Stop between floors," he said, hardly bothering to waggle his eyebrows.

"It happens," said Claire, because it did.

An endless twenty seconds went by. He said, "Can you even imagine doing the stairs?"

"No."

"Nor I."

Claire stared at the green tile floor. It could have been the floor of a hospital. She waited maybe ten seconds more before asking, "You know what they say about puns?"

Brow knit, he looked down, pretending to think. "Ummm." Then back up, meeting her eyes. "No?" His eyes twinkled. He didn't give a shit.

Miraculously, the yellow number was now 10, now 9.

Claire asked, "You know the second floor? That gym there?"

"I do."

"The shower rooms over on the left? That lock?"

"I do." Smile hardly rising, even his anticipation lazy.

The doors slide apart with their expected sound. Stepping in, Claire can feel her chafe lines, can only imagine how they'll blaze. She knows some things for certain, and makes a list. She knows this guy's stomach will be clammy on her. She knows that any pleasure will stand no chance against the pain. She knows that, once she gains her unworthiness, Bo can ask, and she can say yes.

HELLO:

I DO INTEND TO COME BACK, BUT IF YOU'RE READING THIS, I didn't.

    Svaha!

Neeta, if it's you reading this first—who else would it be?—excuse me if I spell your name wrongly, I don't know Tagalog, but if it's you it's the second Monday, which means I've been gone a while, which means my daughter should be called. Tess's number is in the orange notebook I leave here too. Dial 1 first, it's long distance. (She took the scholarship to U. Virginia.)

So, Tess. Where to begin? You probably think I've ignored you, and I probably think you haven't given me much chance, and we are probably both right. But I want to explain myself. What I have discovered about life. It's funny, because I see now that it almost doesn't matter what I say. Words are almost useless. These letters flowing from this pen feel like arbitrary shapes, like language is barely surviving history. But, here:

You can't plan spontaneity, but you can set a stage for it. I found an old gym bag and I'm taking with me a gaff hook, and a peach, and that antique cricket bat of my grandfather's. I chose carefully, though I don't know how, lacking any criteria at all. The gaff hook is rusty and frightening. It could kill someone, including me. The peach, moving around in the bag, is so thin-skinned and vulnerable, so ripe for injury, it makes me wince.

One thing I've learned is that demons, though I call them Protectors, arrive tailored to one's needs. Not desires, needs. You get what you need, as that song says.

What first "clued me in" (that's a nicely compacting bit of old slang for you) happened to be the maniac who attacked me outside the movie theatre, Tess. That night, three years ago now, when I was picking up you and your two friends? You might remember the story because I babbled all about it as you climbed into the car. I was very shaken. You had planned to take a bus or taxi but I was surprising you and forcing a ride on you, trying to be nice and to make up for all the time away, both physically and emotionally, etc, etc, though I knew that you'd be mad and embarrassed, also etc, etc, in front of your friends. In any case, this is what happened that night: I had parked in the mall theatre complex parking lot with a view of the theatre glass doors. I was a half hour early and surrounded by all the empty cars waiting for their owners to finish being entertained, at which point everyone would spill from the doors at once. My plan was to send you an impish mystery text as soon as I spotted you. I had just learned how to enter images and I planned to hide the words of my message between emoticon potted palms. Dad-humour at its worst, but it is our prerogative.

Waiting, I put on the dome light and played the scratch lottery card I had in my inner pocket, something I often kept to reward myself during times of aimless waiting. It was a five-dollar Bingo, with all the features—wild card numbers, hidden treasure icons, six separate games—and quite fun, though it was one of the things I learned to leave behind as a result of this night.

There I sat, mindlessly scratching, focused. Occasionally I'd glance up to the empty glass doors, then back to my game. At some point I heard voices, distant voices to my left, from mid-parking lot, amongst the cars. Loud in the stillness of the night, it sounded like hormonal boys yelling insults at each other, as they do.

I scratched away, barely aware of the voices coming closer, and then it all happened very fast. The yelling was now near enough to make me look up, out my side window, hoping they wouldn't see me and inflict some brutal joshing, "Look at the old fart scratching his scratchy!" or some other witticism, and in the next second here's someone coming right at me, yelling to himself, it was only one guy all along, he strides out from the other cars, hunched, yelling, coming fast. Now he arrived and wrenched open my door and kept coming, screaming, and I screamed back in defence, my forearms and elbows up. His head easily burst through them as he roared hoarsely that he wanted me to *fuck off out of here*. He was stocky, forties, a horrible redhead. I smelled no liquor on his breath though his bucket-mouth screamed inches from my nose. His eyes bugged with a blind intensity I'd not seen before. All this I took in during several seconds of panic. I screamed, *Okay okay* to his screaming at me to leave, and I forced him out with my arms, or he withdrew, and as I found the door handle and got the door closed on him I heard his final ragged bellow: *And quit dialling that number!*

I got the car started and I sped away, simply away, my heart racing ahead of the car. I was moaning. I had wet my pants.

The car was ripe with the clarity that is mistakenly called shock.

Watching the rear-view more than the direction I was heading I exited the parking lot and drove a half mile before I pulled over and stopped, to take in what had just happened. I understood he was a crazy person. Who had misread things. He had seen me scratching at my lottery card there under the car dome's underwater light and mistook this for me intent on a phone, calling someone he didn't want me to call. The man's wife? His doctor? The king of the world?

I saw it all clearly. I saw that he had been too angry to kill me. In his hoarse hysteria he hadn't had enough control of himself to physically hurt me. I remembered yelling at him, *Hey man*, an expression I hadn't used in decades, if ever. I could see his skewed-up face, skin too pale and sick to support even freckles. I had also registered his wrinkles, all of which fed a permanent squint revealing a habitual pain that looked psychiatric.

I caught my breath. My heart slowed. In the trunk I found a towel to sit on. I cracked the window and doubted there was any smell because I was well hydrated that day. I turned back and cautiously re-entered the mall parking lot and positioned the car—doors locked, idling, me looking every way at once—to pick you up, Tess. And on the edge of the fresh crowd there you were, hands slicing the air, talking with your two friends about what must have been a serious film. I phoned rather than texted, no potted palm trees, and you turned and saw me. When I blurted what had happened, you and your friends said, "Wow, intense," and so on but didn't look up much from your phones. Which was fine. But do you remember?

Because I took a lot from the attack. I came to know it as *the wake-up call*. I thought about little else and was on alert for weeks. My state of mind ventured into paranoia, but that was my fault and I reined it in. In the end I found an alertness and readiness that lasted for months, if not longer. That wake-up call was what let me see other calls—so the fruit of that attack, its education, has continued, Tess.

I get ahead of myself. Actually I was damaged for a while. Driving, sitting at the stoplights in a line of cars, I was always afraid and had to twist around to see if anyone was lurching up from behind. Walking downtown streets, or the aisles of a grocery store, approaching any corner I would swing well away, giving myself time to get my arms up if someone came at me.

It took me a while to understand that I was awake, the most awake I'd been in years. It took me even longer to know how to give thanks.

I have no idea what you've learned about me from your mother, Tess, but I've never been a drinker. A bottle of purportedly good scotch whisky, ignored for a decade, I have opened and just now poured a second glass. It won't change anything except maybe lubricate what is meant to be. Not that it matters. In fact a lack of lubrication is often best. A drag of bark over a soft throat will best wake one up to wilderness, for example. But tonight of all nights I find myself drinking.

Once I had cottoned on—now what does *that* mean?—once I was clued in to the basic fact of Protectors, which happened not long after meeting my maniac in the mall, I began to consider the various Protectors I had encountered over the course of my life, without knowing what they were at the time. One of the main discoveries was that they aren't often human. Human Protectors are actually somewhat rare. Or they might be part human. One marvellous example, which had to do with breast milk, changed me so much, Tess—though the story will make you, of all people, cringe at paternal creepiness and ick. Not that I care. Why? Because it might be good for you. Why? Because the story itself might be your Protector.

 Loraine, who I have not seen now in fifteen years, had just given birth to you, and you were not a good suckler at the start. So determined to be the most "natural" mother in the modern world, eschewing not only a hospital birth but anything mechanical—diapers were cloth of course, and guess who had to boil them in a stovetop vat, stirring the dun brew with a wooden paddle like a reluctant wizard? Loraine had taken every breastfeeding herb known to midwifery—basically, breast milk laxatives—and her output was enormous. Tess, you often just wanted to sleep, and that plus your weak sucking resulted in two painfully bloated breasts on your mother. The second day after the birth she was in tremendous discomfort and said, "Come over and get me started." She hoisted her shirt and pointed one at me. The ensuing argument partly had to do with suckling reducing me to an infant, partly to do with her pose in that chair forcing me to my knees, and lastly to do with her "naturalness" and my sense of decency coming into such violent contact that it may well have been what fatally stabbed the zeppelin of our marriage. But that wasn't the demon, at least not for me. The good demon was:

 I did kneel and suck. It took but a second for the revelation to hit me. Again, words are useless here. I'm tempted to say that I lost consciousness, but the truth is that I lost *normal* consciousness and shifted to another kind. Shifted up. It was only later that I understood what happened. In tasting Loraine's colostrum—the thick, healthy goo present in breast milk for the first week, that protects baby from all diseases—I was transported back to the moment I first tasted my mother's breast and the colostrum meant for me. I was shot back to my birth, my first minutes breathing this air. Forty years collapsed to a single second. I was shown the heaven and the hell of time.

I fell from your mother with a shout. I was on my elbows on the floor, hyperventilating. It took a while to convince an impatient wife that I hadn't manufactured another excuse. In the end I did her bidding and went back for more. The Protector's message had already registered, and has remained beyond words. Colostrum, if you're curious, tastes like nothing else. It's like a living metal, like blood but sweeter. You can taste it to the very back of your head.

Tess, I told your mother none of this, which is all you need to hear about our life together. Soon we were happier apart when she went to that invisible place ex-wives go. And took you with her.

Protectors can be mundane. It was a heart attack, not my own, that sparked my understanding. Not long after the mall maniac's attack, with me more alert to the world than I wanted to be, I was idly watching local TV news, a human interest segment.

A marathon runner, a man younger than me, was being interviewed. I heard the words, "The heart attack was a real wake-up call. It changed everything. I'm grateful, actually." He looked so vital, so alert.

Suddenly, being grateful for a heart attack made perfect sense. I began a path of research. Daemons. Kami. Guardian angels. Cultures that believe the world talks to you and gives instruction. (Our culture calls this schizophrenia.) Cultures that have made a hopeful science out of what we'd call luck—the rain dance, prayer, sacrifice, etc. I found it all mostly interesting rather than evidence of anything true. But there was *something* being got at, a kind of unpredictable force at large, doing something to us and for us. Again, it doesn't matter what I think or say about it, it happens regardless. The closest I got to a nearly sensible theory about a *force working on our behalf* was my reading in Tibetan Buddhism, especially the traditional texts that include a good dose of the old nature religion of Bon. The chants, still done by followers today, make much mention of spirits. Dralas, gyelgongs, duns, senmos. There are beneficial spirits, malevolent spirits, spirits of rivers, of mountains and even of the milk pail. These spirits are prayed to, or chanted to, or actually *negotiated* with, the idea being that if they are moved at all, it is due not to your words but the attitude you steep them in. There is a special category of spirit whose modus is to give us a slap. Their sole purpose is to promote our wakefulness. They are called Protectors.

A Protector might be your TV dying suddenly, maddeningly. Or a simple stubbed toe. A rub of your eyes after you've cut jalapeños. Or it might be a fatally leaking boat. It might be cancer. It might be a rotten step on your ladder. It might be a glass door so clean that you walk into it. It might be a head-on collision.

That's so interesting, and beyond irony: your Protector might kill you. According to the Tibetans, we should respond with an attitude of thanks. We should thank them for rousing us from our waking dream.

They are beautiful Tess! I saw a tanka painting of one that has a beard shooting sparks from the tip of each hair, and his gaze is said to set the past, present and future on fire!

The human ones fascinate me most—maybe it's only because they have eyes. Last winter I met another one like the maniac, but funnier. He still makes me laugh—but that might be this scotch, which gets smoother and smoother, I think because it kills any new throat nerve it meets each time it goes down. But, the Santa man. What happened was this: A winter dusk, I walked the sidewalk across from our newly abandoned Target store. I wore my nice dark wool coat, an umbrella tucked under an arm. I resembled some kind of "gentleman." I'm thinking specifically of the Santa in the black and white version of *Miracle on 34th Street*, when he's in his suit-and-tie camouflage, as it were. The point being, I think it was my appearance that brought on his choice of words. Because, out of nowhere—it's always out of nowhere—behind my left shoulder someone sang loudly, sarcastically, the words, "*Right down Santa Claus Lane.*" Then a man on a bicycle brushed past me so close that his elbow hit my ear. Having passed, he then stood up on his pedals, raised one leg and kicked a booted foot straight out to the side, exactly the height of my head, to show me that this is what he could have done. He sat back down and pedalled off. The bike was old and too small for him. The end of each handlebar had an ice skate jammed onto it.

What a thing! He saw my grey hair. You don't ride a bike on a sidewalk and brush past an old gentleman and demonstrate kicking him in the head—you just don't. And that line from the silly carol, to announce himself. Perhaps weirdest of all, to the last word, "lane," he gave a bit of excellent vibrato.

Did he know what he was doing for me? Of course he didn't. Maybe he felt something. Maybe if I had him down with my foot on his neck and asked him in the right way, he might answer that it had "felt right." Or even a "you deserved it." A kind of rightness, in any case. Something beyond him, like he cooperated with an urge. That's my suspicion.

With fantasies of a foot on his neck, I did try to follow him. Not for long, and not seriously, because he looked well built and in his twenties or thirties, and he had disappeared over a hill. But I followed in other ways, checking public ice-skating times at the local arena and then lying in wait—no, who would "lie" in wait?—I waited in the recess of the Target storefront, eyes peeled (!) for a sidewalk biker with skates jammed onto his handles. It was while standing against the red cement of Target that, picturing how I'd spring out to topple a bike and the sounds I might make while inflicting the sort of injury that would make my escape less urgent—it was here that I considered the possibility of being a Protector myself. More precisely, a Protector's vessel.

The moment I saw this, I was instantly and deeply alert. The shocking idea of becoming a Protector *was* a Protector.

First I saw I had to wise up. I had to come down from the sugary thoughts of revenge. Because I also saw:

It has to do with Love. Not love but Love. It might look like a strangest love but it comes from its wellspring, from the fount of Beneficence. Again, I'm not trying to convince you. It doesn't matter what I say. No matter what I say, Protectors will do what they do. To you. For you.

Love. The force invisible to us is Love. If I open to the glow of its invisibility I have a chance of connecting to it, welcoming it, a chance to be a harbinger of Love, the Love that ushers Awakenment, a diamond wakefulness that is our birthright, Tess, and through this Love, if I am lucky, I can undo the holes and endless mistakes and vacancies of my life, and if I am so lucky I will no longer have to apologize, Tess. Even to myself. I want you to know this most of all.

Though because it doesn't matter what I say, I don't care what I say.

I've just cried. A tear fell here:

Just know that we have encountered Love, in these demons, throughout our lives. We all have. Some we forget. Or remember falsely. We hang daisies on the wolf's face. Or we make a wolf of a beautiful daisy!

I don't know what terrorists are. I don't think they are Protectors. Not exactly.

It has to be more than just terrible surprise. Tonight, I hope, a moment will come and I will know. Human Protectors don't know what they're doing. I see that much. They're crazy or awful or explosive, out of touch with consensus reality simply because they are above and beyond it. They do not know what they are doing and that's the point. Their aim is higher than they themselves can know. They are spontaneous tools for the Force that is of benefit to all beings. Of benefit to any who can *wake up during the display.*

Just now I remember the seagull. I was young, your age. I was driving, in a line of cars creeping through a school zone, and for no reason a seagull flew into my windshield. It would have hit my face had the glass not been there. I can so clearly see its flapping wings and open beak and bingbong eyes, going crazy and hard against that glass just inches away. It fell away to the ground and died under the wheel of the car behind me. The driver of that car, I can still see him "laughing with horror," yes, and I wondered then and I wonder now if the Protector was for him, or for me. Or, for you, now, if the cacophony of a dying seagull story makes you hear and puts you more fully into the quiet of the room you are in. Maybe you're in this room, Tess, reading in this kitchen. Can you hear the whole quiet?

I'm talking too much and beyond myself. Words won't do. Won't *do*. That's the point of the Protectors. They use action. They drill a message into your spirit. They drill a diamond with a diamond. It doesn't matter what I say at all! Not even to myself. I'm about to join the realm beyond words. Or try to. I know that my uppity presumption will itself invite a few minor hairy protectors. Ha ha taboo pig sticker boo radley's knife, etc, etc.

I feel sparks spark out from my invisible beard. I can see through the fire in my eyes.

We're everywhere. Yes I flatter myself. No I don't—if you're reading this, Neeta, or Tess, or Officer Poobah, or did you make a trip and are partaking of this too, Loraine—it means I didn't come back and I'm out there still, I'm out there, maybe unlocated, who knows in what shape! Perhaps you've read about me. But I keep flattering myself. I'm no longer to be taken seriously or literally and it's not because scotch has scraped all caution from all words and to have them just tumbling out, look at them all, piggledee-pock pebbles out my head.

It's time. I will pluck that bat-black windbreaker from the peg, pull it on and presto. It's after midnight. I'm not making light when I say I feel like a hero. Into the gym bag I'll add this scotch, half full, half gone, to nest beside the gaff hook, the peach, the old cricket bat. I have no idea how they will be used.

Ready?

OSCAR PETERSON'S WARM BROWN BENCH

I'M SO OLD I WANT TO SAY THIS WHILE I CAN, AND ALSO because the times seem right, with so much fresh racism blooming despite the Obama miracle, with killings by cops and rumours of walls, and elsewhere dark-skinned people forced into boats to wash up on light-skinned shores where they're grimly accepted or shoved back to sea depending on how the stars line up or which way some votes blow.

I don't half know how to say what I want to say but I fear racial conflagrations. The saddest marks of our history have been these. I'm old enough to remember World War II bang shut when two bombs went off, events that for most people remain an icon of retribution, not racism. When I had to tell students that Vietnam came *after* WWII, they didn't care enough to be surprised, nor would they hear that the big politics lurching at them today were shaped absolutely by the difference between those wars. They did know the Gulf shitstorm swelled up more recently, if only because it persists in its various shapes and sizes.

Their opinions on it quickly went sideways with half-baked ideas, as in, Arabs can't do democracy and to stay civil need a ruthless beast with a biggest stick.

I do ramble and will shift gears and steer at Oscar, and my satori moment.

I'm so old I came of age with the Beats and was in fact a wanna-Beat and came to resemble them—for example, I think of satori moments. When I got to San Francisco to sign up it was already pretty much over, which is the nature of any golden age, with its gods having flown and interlopers arriving to scrape at any residual gold, turning things to tin, to dirt 'n' flowers, so to become a hippie movement—I make light. But except for the bookstore-bound Ferlinghetti and others too ecstatic to flee, true Beats were on the road in Big Sur or Algiers or even Japan, incubating the western Zen egg a bit more. I stuck around the Bay and learned to play an earnest jazz piano. But you want to know something about the Beats? They were pretty much a white boys' club.

Anyway, Jane dumped me for Alison. Shedding tin, dirt 'n' flowers, I fled north. I didn't hitchhike, I had a car—unlike a real Beat I kept one foot in and one out. Case in point, I got a steady job teaching music at a high school in Kitsilano, before it became Kitsilano. There, a piano was my only love. Its string of rectangular bones was the radiant spine of life, pulsing everything Darwin and Buddha imagined and more.

There's nothing to say about Vancouver except what helps describe my racism. I won't try to explain it. Why explain walking, or breathing? It might come as a shock when I call racism *natural*. Well, many bad things are natural: planet-killing meteors, malaria, the smell of shit. If racism isn't natural, why does it squat in history from then to now? I think we should take a deep breath, let it out slowly and admit it. Let's be good alcoholics and admit the problem. Let's call a spade a spade. All together now, racism is *natural*. A person's surprising skin shouts *other* at you. *Other* puts the *X* in xenophobe. Burroughs called such a thing a war between the cells. In Vancouver in the early sixties, meeting a black man on a sunny street was literally a shock to the system.

I also think sexism is natural, and homophobia too, for all the same reasons and beatable in the same way. And sometimes you get handed a gift, which is what happened to me.

My encounter with the pianist took place in Australia, but I'm not there yet. I stayed in Vancouver a decade teaching high school music, otherwise noodling morosely on my keyboard, head to one side like a poem-sick James Dean. I didn't have the chops. Why couldn't I play the heart, the gleam, the war between my cells? I couldn't find the rattle, I couldn't do the density.

In the grubby centre of Vancouver lived the Chinese. They cooked us great food, sold us our corner snacks and smokes and were mostly quiet doing it. But on a Chinatown evening, from upper windows weird Asian laughter sugared the alley skies as tiles or dice clicked and snapped. Were they drinking? They stayed mysterious. Two solitudes, Canada was already good at that. In Vancouver there were three: the East Indians lived in

Surrey. Their older men had proud posture and seemed to think they were better than you! I loved their food too. Anyone who conjures a moist tandoori can be as arrogant as they want.

I remember never even shaking hands, never touching the skin of either race. Thinking to give my piano more bingo I once bought some dried ginseng in a stinky shop in the darkest middle of Chinatown, and when the old guy slid me my root wrapped in paper tied with string he made a muscleman pose, indicating the herb's properties, and we both grinned and nodded, our foreheads maybe a foot apart, and some jerky bowing, though that would be Japanese, but anyway that's as close to touch as we got.

This gets me to Oscar. Sometime late seventies Vicky split and the explosion blew me all the way to Australia. I think I sought the revenge of making myself unreachable. Back then the other side of the world could still do that. There was no internet, and a call cost a day's pay. Not many Canadians roamed Oz yet.

Australia was entirely uncool. People looked friendly out of desperation—that isolation and that heat. I couldn't help seeing above each hot smile a face descended from criminals. The buildings were new and tasteless, like Canada, but more sterile in that sun. Like Canada it had bad normal food but good Chinese. When I think Australia, I think hot, hot workplace, and chalk. Yes, I taught. But even nature felt like a hot, hot workplace, just without walls or ceiling. When I did get to see them, those kangaroos and koalas and goofy bright birds somehow just stayed unreal. I'd already seen them on TV.

Canada was uncool too if you didn't know where to go, so maybe that was the problem. I didn't know what golden age blossomed in what cheap cafe. I didn't even know what to look for, being over the countercultural hill. In Sydney I probably thought a buzzcut punk was some farm kid lost in town. And I'll just say one more thing about Australia: Australia was big-time racism with the heat turned up.

Its black people lay about, drunk and penniless in the street, if they happened to wander within city limits. Blackfellas. They lacked even a ghetto. I didn't learn till later that I was seeing the passive endgame of a genocide. I also found out that Aborigines weren't technically black but Indian, or as we would have it East Indian, descended from land bridge travellers circa a long, long time ago. Which is interesting because it meant Oz had whites, Asians and East Indians, the three solitudes of Vancouver.

I had two jobs: playing piano by night and teaching poetry by day.

I've just exaggerated twice. The poetry teaching was actually my fantasy. My reality was teaching ESL—*It is very hot, may I have a glass of water please, that's a fair dinkum automobile Mr. Capone*—to the influx of Asians trickling down like sad rain from the north. We're talking hard times not just in Vietnam, but Cambodia and Laos and Burma too. I was a trained high school teacher who spoke a more palatable tongue than the inimitable Aussies themselves, so I was hired. *What ship did your grandfelons arrive on, Bruce?* I had to tiptoe my bad wit out of trouble a few times.

I exaggerated the piano-playing job by calling it a job. I was up till two most mornings playing through drunken chatter, getting paid the barest minimum the owner could get away with, having guessed rightly that I would've done it for free. The Sandwich Shop was the jazz club where I met Oscar Peterson and he bought me a zombie. I was mute with adoration and hadn't slept in anticipation of meeting him, and the drink was just to get me to say something. Or he smelled poverty coming off me like a bad memory. Not that Oscar was ever poor, to my knowledge. It's somehow hard to imagine a huge eloquent black man named Oscar being poor.

Midnight piano left me too tired to teach well, but I was paid simply to stand there and talk and listen. And harbour a fantasy that I was teaching poetry. My excuse to myself was, since these people sitting before me dead-eyed and heartbroken were here due to dark circumstances, the music of language would cheer them up. I didn't see at the time that I was probably causing harm, but my students took some odd notions out into a frightening world. Chicken was "yardbird," cars were "hot rods," a wife a "main squeeze" and a husband "my old man." I was hot and bored. When a few started pronouncing the punctuation—*Please I want to buy apples comma flour maybe comma and cinnamon*—I didn't correct them.

My classes often went nowhere and I was cheating them. They needed words to help them find a course for apprentice electricians, or directions to the public toilet, and I was not seeing their dire straits because I wasn't seeing *them*. Individuals comma as unique as me. I have been working up to this main admission: *They all looked the same.* I wasn't moved to know their differences.

I remember one kid, one day. I was riffing at compound words that described people's jobs—fireman, policeman, metermaid—thinking that if we made up our own but with real names, it would be poetry. Sparky Sam, Billyclub Bob, Parkinglot Jane. Funny okay!

The boy, maybe sixteen, but so thin he could have been ten years older, hadn't said much in the weeks he'd been in class. But today he sat straighter and announced, "Gendarme!"

It took me a second to realize this was French. Policeman. I recalled that Vietnam had been sort of colonized by the French.

"That's right," I said. "'Man of weapons.' But remember that the goal is specificity and—"

"Weapon Man!"

"That's good, yes. Weapon Man. But it has to be *specific*. So, what *kind* of weapon. Machinegun Man is better. And what specific *man*? So, Machinegun Charlie? Or, you know, there was Pistol Pete. There's—"

"Weapon Man!"

"That's good, sure. Like a superhero. But even superheroes are specific. There's Spiderman, and, you know Superman, and—"

"Weapon Man!"

"Well, no, that doesn't really work, you know, because …"

I avoided the kid's eager eyes, which thanks to me were fading back to dead. Here I was arguing points of poetry with a kid who knew no English, whose life was unfathomable to me, and whose facial scars, I saw now, ran from his upper check to just below his chin.

I realized I was in a confused kind of hell. That the kid was in a hell too, and one way worse than mine, might have occurred to me, but why consider a life you couldn't understand, let alone fix? No, it was just me there in that classroom, alone. A bad teacher. Who at night played a yearning sad-sack piano, and not well. It was sad-sack and yearning *because* it was no good, my fingers ashamed of themselves as they moved. So as I sat there on my piano bench, sometimes solo and sometimes with sidemen— Dave on drums, taller Dave on stand-up bass—I played music that was sad only because it was bad.

The Sandwich Shop looked like a windowless American steak house, all red and black and wrought iron. In fact, steaks were a mainstay on the menu. Mostly it was a booze trough. The patrons ranged from grim old punters to fresh-eyed women here for a hep and dangerous time. It was a jazz club, after all. If Oz had a mafia, they operated out of The Sandwich Shop. The main office had a bulletproof door, and goons slid in carrying hard secrets and small brown paper bags to Mr. Green. Since the place was rarely ever half full, I figured it had to have a hidden source of income, especially when rumour became reality and Oscar Peterson and his group were being flown in for a five-night gig.

I've rambled but I need to say that Oscar Peterson was a hero. Oscar Chops. Fingers Fatman. Weapon Man! He was better than good and I was only bad. He was so black and I was so white.

The night Mr. Green explained the schedule for Oscar's visit, both Daves said a soft "fuck" and looked down. I couldn't speak at all. Because "Mr. Peterson would prefer not to stay up late," he and his group would perform the first show and we would follow and play out the night. Daves and I knew what this would look like. Following Oscar Peterson, our lack of talent would only scream louder. Not only that, but as we tripped through our first measures we would suffer the scraping chairs and maybe catcalls as a true jazz audience got up to leave.

We practised hard for the three weeks we had left. We did light up a few numbers but of course we didn't get *better*. Because we played standards that were in Oscar's repertoire, and fearing we'd find ourselves playing a song he'd just played (which might be funny, as in, So folks, that was how gods do it, now here are some tortoises), I knocked on the bulletproof door and asked Mr. Green if Mr. Peterson had by any chance sent a set list. Mr. Green did a double take for I think humorous purposes, then closed the door in my face. I yelled a plaintive, "Ain't Misbehavin'"? into the riveted metal. "Tenderly"?

Oscar and his men arrived in town. They had been prowling the neighbourhood, having played wacky Japan and square Singapore, and by now I was so afraid of the man that I believe I hated him. From the back of the club, reading my newspaper like a spy, I watched him walk in with his players—they were two white fellas, and this didn't help at all. I studied him shaking hands with Mr. Green, who hunched and writhed like he was greeting an emperor. Oscar was a big man, a big fat man, but he moved like a relaxed cat, so much so that for the first time I saw why they'd been calling themselves cats. He had a huge round pie with big eyes, and his skinny moustache divided it in half. He didn't look human—I'd seen too many pictures of him to allow that. In his dealing with Mr. Green he seemed polite and regal. He was Canadian, of course, and that didn't help either. This pianist, this cat Louis Armstrong called "the man with four hands," was *black* black and Canada meant nothing. The name "Oscar" fooled no one. I sat nursing a red wine and watched from the side of my face as he and his boys sat down to the first of five steak dinners on the house. I watched him eat lots of bread, and mop stuff up with it. He didn't finish his meat.

How funny that we met up in racially maybe the weirdest country in the world: its black people were brown people who'd walked down from India to turn black under this sun. Then the white people got shipped here unwanted from Britain, and it's easy to picture them like flaking white pastry in the stinking hold. The whites behaved to the natives like whites did in any new world, and meanwhile the sun keeps everyone rimming the coastline, where sharks and box jellies don't let them stray far into the water either, and inaudible strains of didgeridoo get zuzzy in your brain and under your skin, regardless of its colour.

So we met, that night in The Sandwich Shop. Oscar finished his meal and stood up, already looking at me from across the room. I ducked behind my paper. He was going to come over. Mr. Green must have pointed out the other piano player to him, and he was doing the polite thing.

"I hear you're Canadian."

It was the squeezed voice of a big man, but ordinary as could be. In fact, this was the first ordinary voice I'd heard in Australia. In theory, here was the man who was the most like me. Canadian, a piano player. I lowered my newspaper to a friendly smile. He could see I was nervous, and of course he knew why.

He pulled a chair and sat. He didn't take the chair across from me but beside me. He was close enough to touch. He was so black. I could see the room's lights reflected in the sweat of his forehead. He was a genius. Genius packed every knuckle. Here was the man most like me, but he was utterly the least like me—he was a big fat koan in the flesh. I figured his blood to be red like mine but maybe not, maybe it was angel red, or black as the devil. It was comic that what came out of him next was so Canadian. He said, "Vancouver doesn't have much hockey, now does it?"

So Mr. Green had told him I was from Vancouver. I could only shrug an answer. I really had to settle down, try talking to a black genius.

He said, "How long you been down under, sir?" Still being polite and trying to get something out of me.

"You must be tired from all the flying," I answered, remembering my own flight, the drone and discomfort of which had lasted not a day but a season.

Deadpan, he did the wing-flap joke for me. Then he said, "This body? I'm always tired."

I nodded, thinking he meant his size, when in fact he was referring to the arthritis I didn't yet know about. He was getting good at hiding things, such as, in the many concerts still to come, a left hand going half speed due to a stroke.

I couldn't settle. I knew I should talk piano with him, but how? I could play, toad-like, two of his numbers, "Hymn to Freedom" and "Tippin'." Others I didn't play simply because my fingers couldn't do the minimum necessary. Could I say any of that? Could I show any white belly to that big face? No, I opened my mouth to babble at him an idea I had for a movie. Yes, a movie. Apropos of precisely nothing I said:

"I have this neat idea for a movie about this piano player, this pianist, who gets, who teaches his little son how to play by sitting him on his lap, and then you know scotch-taping the boy's little fingers to the undersides of his own fingers—" I demonstrated, moving my hands like I had littler ones attached beneath them. "—and tapping out notes like that. You know, giving him the feel?"

"Well, that's cool," said Oscar, nodding, then smiling when I looked up at him. "That's a good picture." It was here he waved the waitress over and ordered me a zombie. He didn't smile at what might have been a dry or ironic joke, and I didn't either. I kept talking about my movie.

"Then the story happens. You know, the big-boom-bam of Dad's career, and the kid doesn't really take to it, to the piano, he hates lessons and he rebels, and just doesn't do a follow-in-the-footsteps thing. It's Dad's big life disappointment ..."

"Yeah. Sure. It happens." Nodding away, giving me his full attention. I'm still insane. I should have been asking him about those fills on "Alice in Wonderland," as in, Please explain to me how a human would go about doing that.

"And then the dad is old and he has a stroke, or he goes senile. Anyway no more playing. He can't even talk or walk. So the last scene is the son, who has you know in private actually been plugging away at the keyboard, telling nobody, and getting pretty good, maybe. So what does he do?"

"What does he do. Right." Oscar politely puzzles up his brow.

"He gets the little dad up on his lap. He tapes Dad's fingers under his own."

"Right!"

"It starts slow. He takes Dad through some of those early old songs, so that *we'll* remember. Our hair stands on end and we cry. Then he takes him through some of Dad's own tunes, hard and complex songs, which all along he has been learning and practising. Here's the big son with little old Dad stuck to him like a puppet, arms and hands and fingers banging away, they're really going for it. In Dad's eyes you can't tell if it's fear or, you know, ecstasy."

I stopped talking.

Oscar had been looking at me, not smiling. He said, "That's a good picture."

He looked down at his watch. He stared at it for longer than necessary. We both knew the shitty white player beside him had just walked his own plank and was too crazy for actual conversation.

"Well, sir," he said, his smile professional now, "that sounds like a fine idea for a movie." He looked over his other shoulder, nodding to his boys, whose faces I recognized too. Earlier they'd been reading the newspaper, chuckling at the weird sports section that I knew mentioned hockey not at all. One had said, in a bad French accent, "Où est les Canadiens?" It was winter back there.

Oscar spread his fingers and studied them. Then said, "Time to get to it."

He heaved his body up and got it turned around and walking, in no hurry and so, so cool in the heat. For the first time I noticed that he wore a suit. Of course he did. Black and thick, shiny yet woolly too. Tiny bow tie and tight collar.

The room was by now almost full, with people still coming in, and when the Oscar Peterson Trio started playing, it was so relaxed and cool and understated it was like the furniture itself was playing. The people coming in were playing, and playing as they ordered their first drink. My zombie arrived, its green umbrella and red rum and sweating glass all part of a quiet crazy jazz. It was probably Oscar's idea and it was so classy, Mr. Green not making any intro at all—everyone knew why everyone was here. Then those three made faster magic and it looked like they weren't even trying, the only muscles moving were those that needed to. They were cats, all three of them. They weren't playing jazz, they *were* jazz. I could see they ordered coffee with jazz, they smoked with jazz, and it would be nothing but jazz when they rolled off their lover and snored. Nor would they worry about the problems of the world because their jazz was already on top of that.

I won't continue this riff because you've heard it before, you've heard about artists being their art. So it was, that night in The Sandwich Shop. I watched and forgot myself and grooved, loving the big man and not jealous at all, until I remembered myself, and clenched, and let the demons in: God, you can even hear that *piano's* joy at being played properly for the first time; when my turn comes I'll piss right here in this padded chair; that man is all pizzazz, his players are carrying him; why are my Daves so shitty, there's better players down the street.

And so on. I grooved, I went crazy, I grooved again, then crazy took hold. At the end of each number I'd more or less faint. *This is it*. When they magically began another tune I'd rise in glorious reprieve. I glanced at the Daves a few tables over and saw they were going through exactly similar times. Meeting eyes, none of us could manage a smile.

It had to end and it did. The big black genius turned to us and, his huge body in that thick suit not moving, dipped a head into the sea of applause. A bead of sweat fell from his nose. And another. Then he hoisted himself, stood long enough to take a deep breath and a little fast nod, and the Oscar Peterson Trio ambled off. I sat frozen. Applause held steady then began to die. I was frozen in Australia. Mr. Green thought so little of me and the Daves that he went to his room, no announcement of a break or what might come next. No lights came up. No one said anything to us at all. We eyed each other, wondering what to do. Some people were leaving. Silence grew far too loud. The Daves looked to me as the leader, so I found myself standing. I watched them stand too. They passed me and I followed them, watching one take his seat at the kit and the other lift his bass. Both their faces so pale in the steak house light.

Our first number was to begin with a long bit of solo piano—inquisitive noodling that eventually finds the theme, at which time the Daves leap in at speed. I stood stunned over the keyboard. The white ivory looked like one big key, not fifty-two. I doubted I could find the first note and a second seemed even less likely. Neither Dave would look at me. I heard someone laugh.

I lost my mind and sat down.

The wooden bench was warm. Deeply, endlessly warm. It was warmth not connected to Australia. It was Oscar Peterson's heat. It was his big brown bum warming my little white one.

The rest is predictable, I guess. I didn't play anywhere near as good as the man with four hands, but I did play the best music of my life. You might think I'm crazy and I don't care about that so long as you believe a little of what I say about how one man gave another man some truth.

What happened is, Oscar's heat came as a shock, not an enemy but the opposite of that. I sank into it. Not in a poetic way but a real, physical way. I was simply aware of his warmth warming me. It drew all my attention. I began to play, my attention down there mid-body as opposed to up here head-high. It's a simple secret about art and music and other things too, the body being smarter than the head.

I stayed in Oscar's heat. At keyboard level my hands did what they knew how to do. Not judged or stared at by me, those good old fingers were free so they flew under the radar of a meddling head. Dave and Dave had to work at the pace of a joy that wasn't quite theirs, and they found a worthy, worthy groove, in a night they would remember.

All that poetry I'd yearned to hear live, my fingers played it. They played Jane in her prime, and they found Vicky. They played Canada melting into Australia, a cool torrid zone. They played my boredom and loneliness and lack of a goal in life. They played my cells aware of Oscar's cells, not at war but at love with them. They played the common blood, just as Oscar had played it and left it in the bench, and common blood feels like nothing but love.

Racism is all I wanted to talk about here because it's such a problem. Why did it matter that the bum preheating my bench was brown, deeply dark brown—why does that matter? It matters because it was *Oscar's* colour. Only if we see the solo person, which includes his personal skin and all the troubles it may have visited upon him, can we know and love him. Don't be colour *blind*, be colour *hungry*, colour and more colour, this colour and that colour. There's no black, no white, there's a zillion shades, and everyone's is crazy different lovely.

My only point here is that I never felt what it was to be a black man, but I did feel what it was to be Oscar Peterson.

He surprised me. When I was racist I thought all black men were beaten-down angry and sad. Partway into our set I glanced up from my cool absorption, my body's groove, and there he was, Oscar Peterson, knees wide apart on a chair, elbow at an untouched glass of Aussie beer. He mopped his face with a cloth napkin. I could tell he'd had a good life, a noble day-to-day. Tonight gently nodding to my Daves' pace with his big fat face and calm Canadian smile. He remained in The Sandwich Shop out of politeness but I could see in his angled gaze that he almost liked my jazz. He could hear I was in my body, and when that's the case the music cannot be bad. It was slower than his, it took longer to say what needed to be said, but I believe it was a genuinely sadder jazz than his. Amazing, right? A black man nowhere as sad as me.

THE CHURCH OF MANNA, REVELATOR

THAT TRUCKER SURE WAS HUNGRY, JOEL HAD NEVER SEEN anyone fork up a steak like that, head jerking to meet the meat halfway. He must be on a hard schedule, and he probably had no love for what he pulled in his truck. Maybe he didn't even know what he pulled—what kind of life was that? The trucker wasn't huge and monster-armed like truckers on TV, but he had to be a trucker, with that ball cap and bulging little belly. Plus this was a truck stop! Also he looked mean, or at least rural and full of opinions on immigration and the whole enchilada. Joel, who was maybe sort of brown, decided to forgive the trucker, the two of them occupying opposite corners and the only customers at this bright truck stop late on a Saturday night. Joel eyed that steak but waited on his Poutine with Zesty Sauce, which he'd been flabbergasted to see on the menu, here in middle America. Plus he really could not afford a steak. Plus it was one in the morning. Joel nudged his dead phone again. Plus it was *probably* one in the morning.

Knowing it looked stupid, he gripped his knife and fork business ends up. Probably only he could see them quivering. And so here it was. He'd been afraid of this day coming, coming for months, and here it was. That last peek at the bank account left him breathless.

He banged both knife and fork nubs on the table and the trucker looked over. Joel put his utensils down gently. Almost with surprise he saw his map of North America open on the table in front of him. He'd spread it out from force of habit. He wasn't going anywhere else. He closed his eyes to banish his fear.

Today he finished spending his inheritance. The whole thing. As of today, empty pockets. No more cash. His uncle, Roany Biswa, who fifteen months ago died owning two dry cleaning stores, left Joel everything, and as of today Joel had spent it. He still had his Lincoln small-SUV, which he had bought outright, and he still had two credit cards, the black and the pale green, which of course he didn't own at all. Kind of the opposite! He didn't owe much on them yet, but didn't know what he would do with them going forward, other than pay the green one off with the black, and have one devil in his pocket instead of two. Other than that, he didn't know what to do about anything at all. Except, he would sleep in his Lincoln. It was white, like in all the ads.

He gazed upon his good old map. His dead phone held down one curling-up corner, a square dish of sweetener packs anchored another. A third corner pointed up free and fluttered under a ceiling fan he could hear but couldn't see. The fourth corner, Florida, was stiff from an old spill and didn't curl—either up or down!

Joel was sure— Joel was absolutely sure the trucker was choking. He'd stopped chewing. Dropped his fork with a clatter. He was staring straight ahead, rigid. Already pale, now the trucker was white. Blue, in this light. His eyes looked way more worried than was normal. Joel hoisted himself on his chair arms. Should he call the waitress—*Iona* on her chest label—or should he hurry over himself, do what he learned in that course, grab the trucker from behind, get the thumb-knuckle into the plexus and squeeze squeeze *jerk*. But do you grab a guy while he's still sitting or wait till he staggers up from his chair?

But the trucker picked up his fork. Then put it down again, took off his ball cap to rub his napkin on his forehead, then looked fast over at Joel, who snapped up his dead phone and thumbed the blank screen. Now the trucker coughed, or actually roared or barked, startling Joel in this empty room. In a crowded noisy bar it was the kind of sound you might not notice, so he decided not to notice it now.

Joel peered into the darkness of his phone, trying to see his icons, but they were hidden under black ice. Or just gone. He had not only cancelled his plan, he left his charger two states back. He could no longer phone or snap or tweet or receive any of same going forward. He had entered the offline life. It would be hard. A guy he met two days ago in a tavern in Montana saw him perform the actual cancellation, saw him use his phone to kill his phone, and he slapped Joel's back and said sorry for eavesdropping Bud but there was a revolution going on, an *off*line revolution, all the kids were doing it, or thinking about it, in all the hippest cities, Brooklyn even, and soon everyone'll be offline and real again, and the hippie and sex revolutions were small potatoes by comparison. The guy was tall and lean with a face identical to that robot in the *Terminator* movie who got shotgun-blasted into mercury blots that re-gathered on the cement and just kept coming. The last thing the guy said before asking Joel to at least buy him a beer, which Joel did, was that the revolution started in Norway, because despite what you might think, people were super-cool there.

"*Tell you what?*" The trucker's belt buckle was two feet from Joel's face. "You're gonna stop lookin' at me. *You got that?*"

"Sure! Of course!"

The trucker squinted down, unblinking, to cement his message. He added a wide-eyed head thrust. Then turned away.

"I'm sorry," Joel said, inserting a chuckle, "I didn't know I—"

With a shouted "*Go fuck yourself*," the trucker went not back to his table but to the cash register, where Iona arrived just in time to meet him, eyebrows up and smiling wide. The trucker shouted at her a happy "Ow-*na!*"

Joel's heart was going as he studied his phone super-hard, all the apps he could no longer see but still reminding him of the badges on his green Cub Scout arm, from the one foster that let him do Cubs. But no more Angry Birds, no more Samurai Fruit.

No more Weather Watch, no RoadAhead. He liked to put the Lincoln small-SUV in four-wheel well before he hit any rain.

"Sir? Don't let Finn upset you." Iona was smiling down on him, excited. A bit of beige makeup hung powdery inside a nostril edge. But she had a mother's smile.

"He was the one who was upset!" Joel declared, feeling the shake in his laugh. Outside came a screech of tires and the roar of a car needing a muffler.

"And there he goes," said Iona.

So Finn wasn't a trucker.

She continued, "He's just uncomfortable with folks he don't, let's just say with folks he don't 'know.'" She made finger quotes and Joel wondered if she was calling Finn a racist, and how brown his skin looked in this bright light.

"You'll be wanting this!" Iona clunked down a sweating glass of ice water. "You didn't ask for any, but you'll be wantin' it. Our Poutine with Zesty Sauce is a little spicy." She nudged his shoulder with her elbow. "If ya know what I mean."

"Thank you." He didn't know how anyone could not know what she meant, but gave her his chuckling smile and knowing look. He banished the desire to tell her he'd been in big cities all over the continent during the past year, exploring foods far zestier than their poutine could possibly be.

And he was just Joel Biswa again. In Montana, before cancelling his phone, he'd finalized his second name change, from Joel Doctor back to good old Joel Biswa. What a vanity that "Doctor" had been! And barely a week after the inheritance came through. Though his uncle was dead and burned and couldn't know, what a slap in the face to him, but Joel had figured "Joel Doctor" would let him walk a little taller, shake hands more proudly, and not "hang back in the shadows." And it did help, it was sometimes even awesome and his confidence almost soared. But people sometimes looked at him funny. Plus it was amazing how many people, even smart people who weren't even joking, asked him, "So *are* you a doctor?" Like there was any sense in that. In Florida, did anyone ask Jeb Bush if he *was* a bush? At football memorabilia shows, did his fans ask Joe Montana if he *was* Montana? Still, Doctor was a fine name, and for almost a year, before it got too loud in his mouth to say, it made him happier than the other way around.

Head back, ice cubes rattling cold on his lips, Joel caught himself chugging water again. There was nothing else to do than drink water! So he went to the bathroom, more out of anticipation than anything else. After peeing a little and washing his hands, he smelled his armpits. They weren't that bad but, unbuttoning his shirt to the waist, he slid some pink soap and then some rinse water in there, because this was something he should get good at.

Back at his table he caught himself about to cry again, so he took the long breaths. They almost always worked. Because what was so bad? Wasn't he just back where he started? After all the legal words, his uncle's will had a message just for him, which the lawyer read out: "Joel use it wisely." And Joel silently promised his uncle that he would, then started spending it. Even many months later, when most of the money was gone, he knew he was still being wise whenever he asked himself, "If money can't buy you happiness, what good is it?" It wasn't a stupid idea—some course people even said so. But "he had to find where on earth he wanted to be." He agreed that this was the key.

Now here he sat in a simple chair in a diner in Iowa, smiling a trembly smile because he still didn't know where he wanted to be, on earth. He tapped his finger on the faded map, the paper smooth as leather, on his first spot, the Goldstar all-inclusive just inside Mexico, and he could still feel all that drinking, and every Saturday the old friends leaving on their flights and the new friends arriving, as he lounged in his beach chair under grey thatch watching them spill from the hotel, trying to guess which girls were with and which were not—almost all were with—and it just became a painful place. He did have those two nights with Julie from Calgary. They went on the snorkelling trip, and the horse-riding trip, but both times after sex—she called it the full rhino!—she went back to her room, and when he hinted he might just follow her to Canada, saying it like a wisecrack, she went cold and that was that.

He tapped Seattle, that primo neighbourhood that took just one week to become boring, so cloudy, and no one out on the streets. Then way over in Boston there was that nice apartment-with-water-glimpse, but there was that thing in hot yoga that was too embarrassing to banish and it ruined all of Boston for him too.

All year, he'd had only two nights of full rhino.

But his failure was not about the lack of a girlfriend. It was about—How was it possible—How was it *possible* to go to such good places, to open your wallet at the sight of honest Bisonhide sandals, or the smell of Prawns in Sauce Ambrosia, or the promise of a course in Genuine Heart-Liberation, and to sleep when you want and do three-metre cannonballs into the pool when you want—How was it possible to do all that and still end up feeling mostly bad?

Iona came with his platter. Joel had his eyes clamped and he was breathing harder than he should have been. He was embarrassed to be found like this, and make a waiter wait.

"Can we just—?" First Iona put down another glass of ice water then lifted a corner of his map, trying to flip or fold it, to make room. Joel grabbed up stiff Florida but now the map had too much help, it flapped and went wild and knocked the empty water glass off the table. The shock of ice cubes and bouncing plastic glass had hardly finished and Joel was smushing his stupid map into a ball and chuckling up at Iona apologetically.

She put his food in front of him, saying "Bon appétit," with a wink to her voice that hinted again at the heat of the Zest. Joel was starving but first admired its sizzle-noise, and he loved the rising heat on his face. He forked up one then another gravied fry, and let himself fall to automatic, which he always regretted after it was over, but as he shovelled and as he chewed he could only see how he'd failed again, he'd ended up with fries in phony shitsauce, he'd been attacked by a real-American. He'd lost all his uncle's money. He couldn't find his place in the sun, because he didn't even know what place he was from, he was probably sort of brown but didn't know why because he was adopted, he was fostered, his Uncle Roany Biswa was not really his uncle, he was a good enough fake uncle even though Joel heard him chuckling into the phone once about "all the Joel write-offs." He didn't know where on earth the sun had shone on his real parents, so not only didn't he know who he was, he didn't know *what* he was.

"And how were those first bites?"

Funny to hear these words way out here in the middle of cornfields. The Poutine with Zesty Sauce was not good at all. The fries were dry, the gravy was from a can and the zest was little dabs of Sriracha, which looked like measles on a woodpile.

"Really really good." Joel forked a fry out of its gravy to hold up and show her.

•

IONA WAS AT HIS SIDE WITH ANOTHER WATER, WHICH SHE placed over the cheque. He had slid down his chair, gaze level with his empty plate; he gathered himself up. She turned away, then stopped. She swivelled back. Without seeing her face, Joel could feel her excitement.

"Just tell me if I'm off base. But you seem—"

Joel could feel how his face sagged like a melted candle. He smiled, lifting it all up for her.

"I'm kind of tired."

"Oh, dear, and don't I see that? But can I ask you a personal question."

"Yes of course."

"Can I recommend a good church?"

"A good church?"

"I'm talkin' about a *good* church."

"They're all good!" Joel tried another smile. On his cheek he felt a clinging cold tear and he knew Iona could see it and it was a big part of this conversation.

"Well then I mean a special one." She looked away to say what she said next. "Do you go to church? Or, a temple, or—?" In her voice was her discomfort about him possibly being brown.

Did he go to church? During his California swing he signed up for courses that were pretty church-like. One place, under huge, huge trees tossed by wind up top but no wind below, they'd prayed. Not to God but to their own love, to make it swell up within. That was also where he learned to banish.

"No."

"Well sir. You're in for a treat." She cleared his empty platter, beaming. "And don't bother eatin' lunch." She raised her eyebrows, which were odd to look at, tattoos maybe. "If ya know what I mean."

This time he didn't know what she meant.

She returned with the pay machine and to give him directions to Gloeville, which she pronounced Gluvul, on whose southern outskirts could be found the Church of Manna. While she spoke, and keyed numbers into the machine, Joel could see that her eyebrows were not only brown tattoos, but that each one had a tiny design in it, a tiny eye. This waitress was always looking at you.

"You heard of manna from heaven, sir?"

"I have, yes."

"Well that's the place for it. It truly, truly is." She pointed her chin at his blank phone. "You get maps on that?"

He explained that he no longer did.

On the way out to the Lincoln small-SUV he scanned the parking lot for Finn. It was empty save for the fuel pumps and their bright humming, and the cold of an October night. Morning! In his pocket he pinched the directions Iona wrote on a napkin, taking forever, printing a big "STREET" instead of "st," and "THREE MILES" instead of "3 mi," when he was too tired to banish his irritation. She said it was an hour's drive, through "nothing big as a town." At his car he was happy to see no key mark along a door, no dog shit on the windshield. One night he'd left a back window cracked open and someone had dropped in a horrible condom, which he found days later. He could sort of understand why fine cars were targets. It was somehow like why brown people were targets.

Joel tossed the phone on the passenger seat. He should have left it, as a tip. One course had said that he must let go of all he had. His life would blossom only then. They did ask for some of it, but they seemed serious that his future waited on the time when everything he owned was finally gone. It was a weird hope to have—that everything would then fly up from nothing.

•

JOEL WAS NOT A BIG PERSON, BUT THE LINCOLN SMALL-SUV was as described. Trying to sleep, he kept pushing the electric button to make the seat go flatter until the tiny motor clicked and clicked then started to whine like an insect in pain. Plus there was nowhere in the church parking lot to escape the bright porch light over the sign, *Church of Manna, Revelator.*

So he didn't sleep much at all. This morning as he pressed the sister button to get the seat back up to normal, he tried to banish his anger at the church because he hadn't given it a chance yet. But he couldn't banish his anger because it was another anger trying to do the banishing, and this anger was also impatient because he had to pee so badly. He forced himself to breathe and calm down. It was good for a church to keep a bright night light, a night light was a proper symbol for a church and what they wanted to do to you. Okay. He grabbed his phone to check the time but he'd forgotten again that it was dead. It was but a black rectangle, heavier in his hand than it seemed it should be.

He turned the car key two clicks and to a chorus of bells he read that it was 9:17. So he'd slept longer than he thought. Which made him feel a bit better. Less angry, anyway. But he really had to pee. And he was really hungry.

It was cold in the forest. Joel had to walk it felt like forever to find a spot behind enough trees where he couldn't see the church so nobody could see him back. It felt great to pee, but he realized he lacked a coat warm enough for the weather that was coming, depending on where he ended up. He could no longer just go to the next department store and buy whatever coat he liked. Well, he could, with the black card, but that felt dangerous. Strange how a thin piece of plastic could feel like a bottomless canyon. Not a dark bottomless canyon, but one where all the lights were on and aiming at you.

As Joel walked through the trees back to his car, hugging himself, the canyon-of-debt feeling helped him decide he wasn't so hungry after all. In his teeth he could suck traces of poutine grease, plus some faint zestiness, enough to make food unessential for now.

But then with a burst of joy that made him leap a step and hiss *yes*, he remembered Iona's words, to not bother eating lunch if you know what I mean!

He heard the crunch of gravel and when he was back in view of the parking lot another vehicle was there, a pickup truck. The door slammed and a black man disappeared around back of the church. The janitor, probably, here to get things ready.

Joel stopped walking. He closed his eyes. The *janitor*? Had he assumed that man a janitor because he was the first one here, or had he assumed him a janitor because he was black? Wouldn't the first man here be the minister?

Joel reached his car in a funk he knew he was helpless to banish. He climbed back into his car, its chiming welcome doing nothing for him, so it went silent to let him sit in his mood. He sat and sat, unable to banish a thing. He'd learned nothing in a year other than how to spend all his uncle's money, so he decided to sit without moving, for as long as he could.

He gazed down the long white hood of his car and thought something he hadn't thought of yet: how happy Uncle Roany was with *his* money. He remembered the day Uncle came home with a new car, his first new car ever, he told young Joel, who hadn't been fostered with him long. He remembered Uncle Roany standing at the front window admiring the white car parked out on the street, how he laughed and went back on his heels and said softly, rolling his *R*s like he did, "The Great Satan." Uncle Roany was browner than Joel. He had grown up in Egypt.

Other cars were arriving and crunching to parking spots. People got out and lifted a hand to one another, though Joel could not hear what they were saying, protected from their voices by his executive car. He banished the selfish wish that nothing like that rusty pickup would park too close beside him and open its door carelessly. He watched people amble in. He didn't see Iona. Or Finn.

Joel waited until all had gone inside and he was alone in the parking lot again, except now it was full of cars. He waited a little longer. Running fingers through his hair in the rear-view and grabbing his phone and keys, he scrambled out of his Lincoln small-SUV. He trotted to the front doors, eyeing the *Church of Manna, Revelator*, whose letters looked homemade, one "n" paler than the "n" beside it. He smelled smoke and saw a waft coming from around back. He heard snapping. Crackling, popping.

He trotted along the side of the church and though the words were muffled he could hear an amplified voice droning within. He turned the corner and found a feisty bonfire in its young stages, a mound of fresh wood chunks licked by under-fire, barely charred. It sounded like eager breath. Above the flames a big homemade spit, its turn-handle made out of a cut up hockey stick. Off to the side an old bathtub, and beside that a big blue tarp, anchored by stones. Everything looked well used.

Joel hurried back to the front doors and pushed in as quietly as he could.

"... and He will provide what thou dost need, and what thou dost seek, gazing hungrily unto heaven ..."

Though the amplified voice was loud, a few people heard Joel and turned. One little girl, maybe five, knit her brow instructively and put a finger to her lips.

He had a sudden inspiration, a burst of hope. The sound of this bored voice, the sight of these faces—sullen or constant-smile or bored—made him realize that this was a good old American church. It was nothing like the hugging yoga and liberation groups.

He'd never considered old school!

The layout was a surprise. Maybe thirty folding chairs circled a glaring empty spot in the middle. The empty spot was big enough for two people to arm-wrestle, or slow dance if they didn't move around. The chairs went back five or six deep, with a few aisles cutting through.

"... and thus He sayeth unto—Neighbour, will you please take a seat? We'd all like to start."

Joel hunched and stepped quickly down an aisle to the first empty seat he could see, which to his horror was all the way at the very front. Eyes were on him and he felt like no neighbour. He felt browner than ever. He sat and stared only at the floor because when he raised his eyes he was looking right at the old lady who was definitely staring at him. If he slid forward in his chair and stuck out his legs he could probably touch her toes with his. She was wearing an elegant but odd suit, the colour of buttery cream. He saw now why it looked odd: the leg cuffs were rolled up, showing their matching satin lining.

"... and put to purposes that ye well know. But under Him, who delivers unto thee ..."

It was a loudspeaker and Joel couldn't see where the speaker was. You could easily hear when a word was in capitals. Joel tried to ascertain if it was a black man's voice or not-a-black-man's voice, and could not.

"... for that which He delivers unto you be not food alone, though it be food. It is also the meat and blood of His own body ..."

The church was hard to explore by moving just his eyes, so Joel turned his head super-slowly so people might not notice. He didn't want that voice to single him out again. The congregation—that was the word—looked to be of all stripes. A few were dressed up but most were not. Some looked poor. Including the little kids and one baby and himself, they were twenty-three. A scatter of old people, one with a walker parked in the aisle. The church had a high, peaked ceiling, which made it feel emptier than it actually was.

"... so let it be said that none other than *truth* shall He deliver unto you from Heaven in which He dwells, and that lo, it is none other than the sustenance in which our own body finds life ..."

In their faces Joel could see they'd heard these words before. He spotted the loudspeaker hanging in a far corner, an old wood box painted the colour of the wall, brown. Finally Joel identified the smell in here. For sure it was potato salad. And he could smell coffee now too. Joel really wanted some coffee. And then the thought of coffee made him need to go to the bathroom. Which made him understand that he hadn't done that particular business for a day or more. Nor had he brushed his teeth. He was no doubt a horrible sight and he probably smelled. He *was* horrible. Sitting in these folks' church.

They kept quickly looking up, especially the children. They looked up, then down. He looked up too and saw it. Suspended from the ceiling directly above was a huge box, a small room really, painted the same brown as everything else. A metal walkway, supported by rafters, led to the room from the back end of the church. From what he could see, the room was windowless, just a box. But in its floor, directly over his head, were the lines of a trap door.

And it was starting to open, slowly, like a squeaky drawbridge opening down. Like a lower jaw opening to let something crawl out of a mouth. The voice took on a more musical tone, like a chant. Joel had heard these words already. And now the congregation, or some of them, were repeating the words too.

"... from Heaven unto you is not food alone though it be food. It is also the meat and blood of His own body, and so it be truth ... Descending from Heaven unto you is not food alone though it be food. It is also ..."

The old woman across from him spoke the words boldly, her voice strangely deep, and though Joel wouldn't look at her directly he could tell she still stared at him. Most others mumbled the words and looked this way and that with, Joel thought, some embarrassment. Kids stared up ceaselessly, which forced their mouths half open, and they didn't seem to care what sounds they were making.

Descending now on a thin yellow rope, then falling so fast Joel flinched back in his chair to get out of the way, was a pouch. It looked old, maybe leather, and grubby with stain. It stopped and bounced and the girl to Joel's left grabbed it, unhooked it from the rope and thrust it at her father, who had some money ready in his fist. He stuffed in what looked like a bill and some change, then passed the pouch along. It moved around the inner circle first, coming to Joel so soon that he barely had time to panic about the quarter and dime he had left in the way of cash. So it was without much thought that he dropped in both coins and also his cell phone, which left an odd bulge. The pouch went behind him and did its rounds. He heard a brief hissed argument between a man and woman, but otherwise all was bright silence. Joel thought he detected a new and piercing smell. The pouch had smelled, actually, and now it was also in the room. Barnyard.

The same little girl hooked the pouch back on, tugged it twice, proudly, then up it shot, at a jerky speed you could tell was hand-over-hand. The bag disappeared into the trap door, which cranked closed. A minute went by, and from above you could hear muffled clatter and what sounded like dropped and rolling coins, but mostly silence. Then the voice over the loudspeaker:

"Not enough."

The trap door opened faster this time and down came the pouch, also faster, in fact it basically dropped, looking angry, if a bouncing old pouch could look angry. Joel heard grumbling and saw some rolled eyes, and one severe-looking guy, who reminded him of Finn and could have been related, looked plainly pissed off.

The voice said one word, in a whispery, raspy tone, the speaker's mouth too close to the mic.

"*Widdershins.*"

Trying to look as angry as the pouch, the little girl stood briskly and unhooked it, and again, but this time in the opposite direction, the pouch made its rounds.

Joel had to go to the bathroom and he was starving. He felt the contradiction of this—desperate to shit, he was also desperate to eat—as cruel. He wanted all these complications to be over. He wanted this, that and everything to be over. He felt on the verge of whimpering, just whimpering an endless growing stream of sound that might not stop, but the old lady was staring at him, and the little angry girl with the smelly pouch nudged his shoulder, and then she punched it—only now did he know the step he must take.

When he took the pouch from her he was ready. In went both his black card and the keys to the Lincoln small-SUV.

So that was that.

The old bag jerked skyward on its yellow rope. The trap door closed. Joel thought he could hear a different silence in that upper room. A judgment. Whatever it was, with the trap door still shut there came a sudden chaos of thuds upon it, and the people around him settled back, looking satisfied.

The door squeaked open again. After brief sounds of struggle and the jangle and croak of a leather harness, four hooves appeared. Lowered slowly, the animal began to turn in the still air. All heads craned up. One little voice said crossly, "We 'ready *had* that."

It descended faster and now Joel could smell it from where he sat, he could smell the goat before he knew it was a goat.

There was a group squeal and one side of the audience flinched as, a second later, droppings just missed the feet and legs of the old woman across from him, who sneered at them heartily. Joel thought of black date pits, and he thought of his uncle.

Still turning in the air, the goat's downward pace slowed as it neared them. It had stopped jerking and kicking and rode stiff in its harness, four legs straight down, looking straight ahead. It bounced down another foot, then another, and then it steadied, right in front of and head high with Joel. It hung, not two feet from his face, turning in the air.

He had never seen goat eyes, not really. They were shaped differently, with a pupil like a cat's, but lying flat, like an alien's. They were empty, yet at the same time deep, and how was that possible? The goat kept turning as it hung in space and its wise face, moving away now, looked coy. And here came its hind end, pungent with piss and straw and waves of heat, just as alive as its face. The smell was so harsh and stinging, Joel could do nothing but close his eyes and wonder if this goat knew they were going to eat it and if it cared, and when the smell eased and he opened his eyes again, he had to shriek and laugh too, because here was the goat eye to eye with him again laughing, it was laughing!

THE RETURN OF COUNT FLATULA

"YES, HELLO."

"Is this Connie Musto?"

"..."

"Connie?"

"May I ask who's calling?"

"Don't recognize the sexy voice? And I know you're not Musto anymore."

"Um. It's Connie Broome now?"

"Hi, Connie. Still can't place the voice?"

"That's not *Bill*, is it? Is this Bill?"

"Think, after Two Rivers High. But before School of Business."

"... Michael?"

"How ya doin', Connie."

"Michael!"

"Long time, no?"

"Oh my God?"

"Long time."

"Well I don't even want to count! It's, it's—"

"Painful to think in decades."

"Well it sure is!"

"Sorry to do that to you."

"Well you're forgiven! Michael! So, where are you?"

"Boo! Look out your window."

"…"

"Gotcha. Sorry. No, I'm still way out here. It seems to be home. Any more west, we get wet."

"You used to say that."

"How long you been in Virginia?"

"It's DC actually, where I 'am.' My office. But I live in Virginia. You know, across that river. How'd you track me down?"

"I don't actually."

"You don't."

"I don't know 'that river'?"

"The Potomac! You don't know the Potomac?"

"The one where George Washington does king of the world?"

"Ha ha! How'd you track me down?"

"I'm a new Facebook person. Just when everyone's leaving—"

"It's all about the tweets and the snaps!"

"It took about five stabs on a button, and there you were. In all your glory. 'Realtor of the Year.'"

"Oh that's such old news."

"And two kids, wow—"

"They are absolutely the light of my life."

"—I knew you'd change your mind. But that main website? You're running for office? Holy cow."

"Oh my God! I'm surprised you even recognized me."

"There you were. Still you."

"That's a horrible picture!"

"If you want me to say you still look like an angel sent from heaven, I will."

"Michael, you're not allowed to flirt—I'm married!"

"Just kidding."

"Well, I know."

"And, 'People Power.' That's brilliant."

"Why, thank you. I do have help. The Constitution, for one. 'We the people'?"

"But it's amazing, how you took an old lefty slogan and flipped it all the way so the right can use it now too."

"I don't like that right-wing, left-wing thinking, Michael. We should not see the world in black and white. We should—"

"I do agree with you there."

"We are united under one flag but we are individuals. We are all *people*."

"What was that other one? 'The do-it-yourself candidate'?"

"'Do it *for* yourself.' Because, Michael? If *you* don't do it, no one else will. Certainly not government. It's the *people* who have to—"

"Right, right. But, okay. Doesn't that sort of say that, once they elect you to be government, they shouldn't expect you to do anything for them?"

"Michael? It's a slogan?"

"Sure, sorry. So you gonna win?"

"Of course I'm gonna win!"

"Well best of luck. That incumbent guy looks pretty dug in. I'll be watching from afar."

"I'm going to win."

"You always were into the positive thinking."

"I actually think it works. I truly do."

"But if everyone trying to get elected, or rich, thinks that way, and almost everyone loses, that sort of disproves it, doesn't it."

"Well, who's the Danny-downer?"

"I'm sorry. Good luck. I'll stop being a downer. But you know I have to say you sound kind of southern? You were always good at doing southern, but now you almost *sound* southern."

"I don't know what to say to that."

"You didn't sound southern right there."

"Okay."

"Do they all still say 'cooter' down in those-there parts?"

"..."

"We're adults, I'm just fooling around. You used to say that word."

"I did not say that word!"

"You did. You completely did. When you drank. You were being funny. You said it softly, like a secret. Your 'cooter.' You liked saying it."

"I don't think I'm going to listen to you anymore."

"I'm not flirting. It's just a cool word. Did you know it actually means turtle?"

"So. What are you up to these days? Still—what was it—still into the chemistry?"

"Oh, not a chance. I mean not professionally. I actually did go on and do some lab stuff, your basic big pharma assembly line. And then, I don't know ..."

"Right, right."

"I was actually a journalist for quite a while."

"Oh, for who? Would I have read you?"

"You might have. You ever read the *New Yorker*?"

"Well I mean *yes*?"

"Never got in there."

"You haven't changed. Still funny as can be!"

"*Mother Jones*?"

"Oh yeah?"

"Got in there a couple times. Kind of your 'organ of the left.' But a noble lady."

"Well that sounds like you."

"A noble lady?"

"Ha, ha. So you're a writer!"

"I'm sort of between things."

"Well it's good to keep your options open. I really do believe that."

"But I'm a man on a mission ..."

"So what's your mission?"

"In a minute. Let's catch up."

"Okay then. And did you get married? Any children?"

"Not really."

"Well, I don't know how to take that."

"That makes two of us."

"Um, so ..."

"Sorry. I'll just, it's been complicated. Picture a wife who didn't want to be a wife. And a kid who didn't want to live in our mess, because what kid would?"

"What kid would. Exactly."

"Then picture a guy who didn't know how to be honest, at the time. That would be me. So was I ever married?"

"Michael. That just sounds so sad."

"That was a long time ago too."

"Right."

"..."

"Michael! So! It's so great to hear from you."

"It must be!"

"Ha ha. No, really, it is."

"So, anyway, I was thinking of you the other day. Don't mean to scare you, so to speak, but you were in my thoughts."

"Well that's nice. It really is."

"So do you remember Count Flatula?"

"Do I remember what?"

"It's this thing we had. It started as 'Flatulent Dracula,' and you came up with 'Count Flatula,' which was obviously way better."

"Um, okay."

"No it started with this thing we saw, the worst thing you could do to someone. It was an adult cartoon or something, and there was this farting vampire. Remember? He was sucking someone's blood, some damsel's blood, and then he farted? While doing it?"

"Hmm!"

"And we decided this was the worst thing you could do, a symbol for the very worst thing you could do: to be basically killing somebody, and not care at all, not a bit. You're killing somebody and in the middle of it you just fart? That's how little you care. The ultimate insult. Complete disrespect."

"I think I do remember …"

"Yeah. It was no big deal but we had the little code name, 'Count Flatula,' and we saw it all over the place, especially in movies, you know, the Dr. Evil type who eats bonbons and yawns while the victim is torn apart by lions sort of thing, and then all the buddy cop shows, you know, *Lethal Weapon*? Shooting someone dead and cracking a joke? At the same time? You know?"

"Well I do. So Michael—"

"*Sorry* to go on like this but this thing in the news yesterday, maybe you saw it? It made me think of you and Count Flatula, it really did. There was this shark attack, this beach south of San Francisco, great white or maybe a bull shark they think, but anyway this guy got nailed, right out of the blue, got grabbed by the *inner thigh* the article said. Holy crap, right?"

"Oh my God?"

"Inner thigh, which I totally think was a euphemism for *private parts*, I'm positive that's what the article was insinuating. This shark basically tore into this poor guy and—"

"Oh my God?"

"—and the worst part was, the shark just spit it out. That's what it said: 'Spit it out.' Tasted it and spit it out and just swam away. No respect whatsoever."

"Well, none! Absolutely."

"Rips a man's *gear* off and just spits it out and goes looking for a tuna or something."

"Count Flatula."

"Exactly."

"Well that's just crazy."

"You were actually the one who was good with words, you know. I said 'Flatulent Dracula,' and you instantly flipped it to 'Count Flatula.' Mine was clumsy, and you just cleaned it right up."

"You have an amazing memory, Michael."

"Oh, I'm an elephant."

"I have to say that this is an odd conversation, but I love it!"

"Me too."

"Michael, how long has it been? Have we seen each other since—"

"You were totally the good one with words. Remember how you'd hear, 'From the bottom of my heart,' and you couldn't help picturing a heart with a bum hanging off it, and you'd always crack up."

"Really?"

"Even as a little kid, you said. You had this—You really had this gift for nailing the clichés. Cutting through innocent expressions that—I remember you telling this guy, this arrogant quarterbacky guy, who was saying he didn't like to toot his own horn, and you interrupted him with this gleam in your eye and you said, 'Well you'd *like* to, but you can't reach it.'"

"Oh I was naughty. I know."

"Anyway, no. We haven't seen each other. Ever since Europe."

"Since Europe. I think that's right."

"Since the airport, actually. I drove you. Let you off in that craziness in front of Departures. Quick kiss and, bang, out the door, and you're off on your 'European adventure.'"

"The Red Tomato! I loved that car!"

"The old Dodge, that's right. With the push-button gears ... And that's right, you called it the Red Tomato."

"It had an eight-track stereo! It was an antique even then. We used to cruise in that thing?"

"That's not all we did in that thing."

"You're flirting."

"I'm just remembering. And that was the last time you saw me, sitting in the Red Tomato. I remember you walked away doing the dramatic 'it's too painful, don't look back' sort of thing."

"Oh my God, that was such a long time ago ..."

"Or maybe you just walked."

"That was such a long, long time ago ..."

"And your one letter. You meeting Yoicheem, etc."

"It was pronounced 'Yoycum,' actually. He was a nice man ... Um, Michael? Do I hear a slight ...? You can't possibly be holding a grudge after all these ..."

"All these decades? Connie? No. I don't. I'm a realist. If I'm anything, that's what I am. I've had a rich life. My decades have been full."

"Europe was such a strange, strange time."

"I'm sure it was. And how you doing, Connie? With your life? Real estate been good to you?"

"It's been good, it's been good. Even with the downturn."

"And your husband. Big Mr. Broome. What's he—?"

"How did you know he was big?"

"I don't know, I guess he has a big guy's face."

"Raymond's a Washington lawyer. He does well. We—Oh he works far too hard, that man. And now with me running for office I swear we have to make dinner dates."

"That can be okay. That can be fun."

"You'd really like him, Michael."

"Oh, but would he like me?"

"Of course! Of course!"

"Just kidding. Hey, Connie, okay. I'm going to hit you with something, right out of the blue. Okay?"

"I don't like the sound of this. Didn't that shark of yours come out of the blue?"

"I'll come out of a different blue."

"Okay."

"It is going to be strange. But honest. Honest from 'the bottom of my heart' honest."

"You're going to visit. Michael? I don't know if that's—"

"I'm not going to visit."

"Okay. And, sorry, I didn't mean—"

"That's alright."

"Of course I'd *love* to see you."

"No worries. No, this is a proposition. I'm going to give you an opportunity, and you can take it or leave it."

"No offence but let me guess? You want to help me get in on the ground floor of something incredible. I'll just say right now I don't do pyramids. Never have, never will. They always sound great."

"Connie? Just listen, alright? And hear me out the whole way?"

"Okay. I'll hear you right out the door."

"You and me. We were going out. Dating, whatever you want to call it. Basically almost living together. For two years."

"We were really young."

"We were young. You, first two years of university. Me, community college. I was also working pretty much full-time."

"It was amazing you had time for me."

"It was amazing. I did think it was amazing. And I thought we were good, and things were fine—"

"And they were!"

"Maybe they were in some ways. But then you decided to go to Europe, and I wasn't invited, because you needed to find yourself and be free—sorry, don't mean to mock. It's all good. It was probably the right thing for you to do, it probably was."

"It probably was."

"The thing is, Connie, I paid your way. I bought your ticket."

"You did?"

"I bought your ticket."

"You bought my ticket."

"I just went and bought it. That's how much—Anyway, I bought you your ticket. And, you know, I bought your traveller's cheques, and your blue backpack, and your *Europe on $10 a Day* book, and sort of ironically I also bought your little yellow money belt ... And, off you went."

"I think I do remember now that that's exactly what you did."

"I did. And so Connie, here's the big honest part. I'm broke, I won't bother telling you why, but I'm more than broke, and I'm giving you the opportunity of righting a wrong and paying me back."

"..."

"That wasn't easy for me to say. But I did, and there it is."

"Well, Michael, you know what? I think I'd be happy to pay you back. I think I would. And with apologies. That would be absolutely fine. I could send you a cheque in the mail, and I could send it tomorrow."

"..."

"Okay?"

"Thank you."

"And, so, okay, how much was it? That *long* ago, a ticket to, a ticket to England, a ticket over the Pole to Heathrow, my God, that couldn't have been all that much I don't think. Four, five hundred dollars?"

"The plane ticket, with taxes, was seven hundred and thirty dollars. The traveller's cheques and other stuff takes it up to two thousand one hundred and fifteen. There was also that pair of hiking boots."

"Well then, okay. Done and done. So ..."

"Connie? If you really want to pay me back, if you want to take full advantage of this opportunity I'm offering you to make things right, I also worked out the interest owing."

"Really!"

"I had someone help me. She calculated it at the yearly going rates, compounded over the twenty-nine-year life of what could have been considered a small business loan. I don't mean to sound cruel, Connie, but charging interest came to mind only because of what you did."

"And what did I do."

"In the middle of what I thought was a good relationship, you took my—"

"It was good!"

"You happily took my money, you let me pay for your European adventure to go find yourself, and that was fine. I came to see that that was totally fine. But then you not only didn't come back, you didn't even bother telling me when you *did* come back, and you wrote me only that one time, about Yoicheem, and I don't even know how many letters I wrote that chased you all over Europe and God knows where, and the single one you wrote to me was just a little note, about you and some guy with a weird name—And you dotted his "i" with a little fucking heart? Do you remember that? So, clearly I was completely wrong about you-and-me, I was clearly living in some kind of big-league delusion. And in the end I did thank you for setting me straight but it took a long time. It was the beginning of my education, the real one—"

"Do you still have that sword, Michael?"

"..."

"Do you remember that sword? For your birthday? It was an antique samurai sword and it cost a lot of money. But I got it because I knew you'd love it. And you did love it. Do you remember your sword?"

"Of course I do."

"Did you love it? I think you loved it."

"Of course I loved it."

"Do you still have it?"

"I sold it. To pay rent or something. Years ago."

"Well you loved my sword."

"I did."

"I gave you things too."

"I loved your sword."

"Good."

"But you know how life is just a dream? And the person you think you're really really close to, and living the same life with, has their own dream? and you share the same can of soup with them, and maybe you even give them a sword, and you ride in the same bench seat of the same red car and drink from the same bottle in the woods, and you even laugh together at other people's stupid dream lives, and you whisper *cooter* back and forth, and lie there between the very same dirty sheets, and it all feels real, it feels nothing but real. But it's worlds apart. It always is. All of us. All us people. Literally worlds apart."

"Not always, Michael."

"We're all individuals, like you say. You were my university education. My wife was grad school. Maybe I'll tell you about it sometime."

"Michael, that sounds so sad."

"You know what's sadder, Connie? You're still dreaming."

"Well I think you're very wrong."

"You still are. We all are."

"You can speak for yourself."

"And I think you probably will win."

"And I truly hope you're right. And now I have to go. But, Michael, when I do I am going to sit down and write you that cheque."

"Okay, whatever, yes. And so then if you're interested—hey, that's the kind of little pun you always had your antennae out for—if you're 'interested' in knowing the entire amount of what you owe me, morally, ethically and I think honestly, and, you know? maybe even *legally*—though that wasn't a threat—the compound *interest* on that European adventure adds up to twenty-seven thousand, two hundred and seventeen dollars and thirty-one cents."

"..."

"Connie? It's the opportunity of a lifetime."

"You don't have to be cruel, Michael. And I will say now that I never did enjoy your sarcasm. It might even have been why I left, now that I think of it. Your *tone*."

"My tone is none of your business now."

"I hear someone laughing there. I can hear someone laughing."

"Connie? I can promise you I have very little laughter in my life."

"Alright, we're done here. Michael? This is all very—All very 'interesting,' there you go—It's interesting, I'll grant you that, and I will sit down and I will discuss this with my husband and I will think about it."

"Ask Big Mr. Broome what he thinks."

"And I'm sad that you are this desperate for money."

"That's also none of your business."

"..."

"You've heard me out the door, and I'm being mean. You sound like a decent person. I guess maybe people change."

"Michael, I think they do."

"Anyway. So I've done it. I've called you. That shark story ... Biting and spitting out some guy's ... Really jogged the old memory."

"Yes. Count Flatula."

"No. You."

CRITIC

LA BELLE CHINOISE HAD OPENED A MONTH AGO, AFTER extensive renovations took it from a failed upscale tapas place to a hopeful French-Chinese fusion. Scanning her overly large, quaintly tasselled menu, in the entrees Valerie read no further than the word "carp." More precisely, *Sustainably farmed grass carp in beurre noir with fennel, garlic and capers.* She had her doubts about the capers/fennel marriage, basically a pickle versus licorice clash unless one or the other was held well back, or the capers weren't blended in but simply scattered on the fish as a kind of beauty mark. When she asked the waiter how fresh the fish was "really and truly," the bespectacled fellow hesitated, nervous in a way that said he knew who she was (they really shouldn't have put so recent a photo on that last cookbook). Or he was deciding how or whether to lie.

Not meeting her eyes he said, "Fresh. Really *and* truly."

So it was the gearing up for impudence that made him nervous. He was a hipster, one approaching middle age at that. Valerie declared to herself that hipsters were *essentially* nervous and that this was, ironically, or even paradoxically, part of their cool. Across from her, Lee sat back and predictably ordered the duck. The waiter turned and left. Val didn't tell Lee about her new understanding of hipsters because he looked to be in a mood to ignore her joke and attack this latest of what he called her "blanket judgments." He didn't let her get away with much. But of all the friends she brought out to eat, Lee was the most appreciative, and probably this was why she asked him most often, or rather he asked her, whenever he was in town. He loved food. He didn't let his ignorance get in the way. He overindulged in drink. He had a cat named Klaatu, the effort behind the name making him, not the cat, seem banal. They'd slept together once, three months ago, her inclination more than his, she still felt. He was younger, significantly so, even at this stage in the game, forty-three to her forty-nine. But on balance she was better looking. All of this still counted, and would show in how they were with each other over this bottle of wine, which was now arriving. Perversely, given her fish order, a beefy red, a rustic Côtes du Rhône.

Lee looked jumpy tonight, something on his mind. Extra energy turned him boyish. He tapped with his knife and kept glancing up and smiling at her for no reason. Maybe he'd closed some big deal. She didn't know exactly what he did but it had to do with real estate, and was international. He was successful, wealthy even, but a big deal still perked him up.

He asked her, "So will I get a bite of your carp? Never had it."

"Not if it's great," Valerie said, smiling to signal the mild joke. They always sampled each other's choice. Lee's opinions were always sought. Sometimes they made it into print. He liked to follow a particular piece of wisdom: "First thought, best thought."

"Have you eaten carp?" he asked.

"A long time ago."

Carp. Valerie couldn't believe how thrilled she was. Actually, the word might be anxious. After this long.

"It's very bony," she said. "I wonder how they'll handle that."

"Maybe they let you handle that."

"I don't think so."

"And if they do, you'll make them pay."

Lee enjoyed teasing her for her ability to bring a new restaurant down, or at least stagger it, with a review. He seemed nervous about this proximity to her power, and afraid she might use it. He had a cute way of praising a bad meal, unaware of how transparent he was.

"I remember reading," he said, "I forget what book of his, but he had this great thing about a bony fish. It was really funny. He's in this jungle and the natives catch a big fish in the river and roast it in a banana leaf, and they're all sitting around hungry, salivating as it cooks, it's like a special food for them or something—Redmond O'Hanlon, you ever read Redmond O'Hanlon?"

"I don't think so, no."

"He's great, he's a travel writer, he's hilarious."

"No."

"So they roast this fish, and he's starving too and he gets some passed to him and he tries it and he says—it's so bony it's like sucking lard from a hairbrush."

Valerie laughed. "That's excellent." She laughed again, imagining sucking lard from a hairbrush. How some writers could write. "I hope tonight I don't have cause to plagiarize that."

"I don't think you will," Lee said somewhat oddly. He smiled as he looked away.

The appetizers arrived. Lee had the "Prawns in Rock Salt 'n' Peppa," which had nice char on them, she could smell it from where she sat, but there were only three and they were not large. When an appetizer was tiny but pushed twenty bucks, it had better be groan-worthy. Valerie had another cheekily dubbed choice, "New Classic French Onion Soup." As soon as she forced her spoon through the top crust of Gruyère she could smell star anise. A reasonable addition to the beef broth, but surprising given the cheese. The onion hadn't been cooked to mush. This might be very good.

"And another …?" Lee asked the departing waiter, pointing his chin at the wine bottle, still a quarter full. He turned to her. "Or should we get something different?" Valerie didn't respond at once, not knowing what to say, so he said, "You're the pro." Then added, "I'm buying, and it's a special occasion." Lee knew her stipend allowed for one mid-range bottle of wine. She wondered what deal he had signed. Over their first meal together she had let him know that she admired a great cook more than a great capitalist, and maybe this was why he still tried to impress her.

Valerie asked Lee to pick one and he said "Oh boy!" grabbing the wine list. He looked good tonight. He had the best hair, a golden bronze, wavy and soft as pollen, no grey yet. He claimed he shampooed it only twice a year and just rinsed it with plain old water whenever he showered. He said hair got greasy if you shampooed it too much, a kind of vicious cycle. She found it a bit hard to believe, but why would someone brag about not using soap? And he knew how to dress—tonight he looked great in navy and black and accents of grey. She still didn't like that he'd had his teeth whitened to an unnatural state—what first came to her was the funny word "hideous"—but she was used to his bright mouth now.

"Let's get this, this, this, and this," he said, stabbing at the wine list. He knit his brow and said, "Or let's see," and turned it upside down.

Where else but in a restaurant were you placed this close, face to face, with someone? Nowhere she could think of. Low light was a fine idea. Did he act up because he felt relaxed with her? Was he so relaxed because he knew she had never been married, had never lived with anyone even, signalling some huge invisible defect? Since sleeping together he had hinted more than once at an encore but never persisted, and she always had the review to write. He was good looking. Eyes maybe a tad close together but otherwise a decently handsome man. And younger. Was he relaxed because he thought he had the upper hand?

"You know that I grew up on the banks of the Seine?" she said, after Lee ordered. She'd been distracted and not listening to his discussion with the waiter, until Lee said "special occasion" again and referenced the film *Sideways*, impish as he asked the waiter for "a Pinot just like that one in *Sideways*." To which the hipster winked, pointed a pistol finger at him, turned on his heel and went for the wine. Who knows what they were going to get.

"The Seine? You're from, you're from—"

"Winnipeg. There's this stream there called the Seine. A tiny muddy thing." She lived on the Saint Boniface side, downwind of the meat packers. It occurred to her only now that whoever named that muddy trickle, a Frenchman of course, had to be a smirking cynic. She used to catch crayfish in the Seine, unaware they were a staple delicacy to the Acadians in the American south. These Seine crayfish were too polluted in any case. Her father called them "crawdads" without irony, not knowing how funny he sounded saying that word.

Lee was looking nervous with her long pauses. She told him what was on her mind. "I actually caught a carp once," she said. "A big one." She said this softly and it wasn't clear that he heard.

•

BESIDES WINTER, WHAT HER FATHER HATED MOST ABOUT Winnipeg was the fishing. The rivers intersecting the city—the Red, the Assiniboine, the tiny Seine—were so polluted that, it was said, if you fell in you'd have to go to the hospital. If he wanted to fish he had to travel. This made him cranky, the mood would grow during the drive and last through the fishing itself. He sometimes took Val. This usually followed her parents' mumbled argument, one Val pretended not to hear. She liked fishing. Mostly, she liked going someplace different. The drives were silent, and through the window she scanned the new scenery in the same way she would read a book.

One day when she was almost fourteen her father drove them east to the Brokenhead River. The Trans-Canada Highway wasn't much in those days, a two-lane road, and they fished right from the highway bridge. Her father leaned with elbows on the rail, rod in his hands, a line of beer cans hidden from view behind his large tackle box. Aside from simple instructions he still wouldn't say much. Val went silent too, pretending that this kind of gruffness was part of fishing. Today the sun was relentless in their faces and they were both squinting. Her heart fell when he muttered to himself, more than once, "I can't *believe* I forgot my hat," not thinking of her, of her eyes, at all. They could hear one coming and had time to prepare, but whenever a semi whooshed by it was more frightening than fun, and knocked her body sideways a few inches and almost into his.

Apparently there were trout and pike in the Brokenhead, and they cast red devil spoons, her father's lure of choice whenever he fished someplace unfamiliar. He was great at casting, and sometimes he'd say, as much to himself as to her, "Right under that branch," or "Over at that rock," then whip his rod, and usually that's where the red devil would *plunk*. Val's casts always landed twenty feet exactly in front of her, which she figured was good enough.

Today they weren't getting anything and Val was soon bored and trying not to show it. She jigged her lure just under the surface directly below, pretending to fish but really seeing if she could get her lure to flash in the dark water, and then how many times in a row she could get it to flash identically.

"Jigging's good," she said to her father, who didn't respond. She added, because he sometimes said this himself, "If it's not working, it's good to try something new."

"It sure is," he said, reaching down for a new beer, and she wondered if it was a joke.

She let too much line out and the lure got snagged on the bottom. Usually she was good at getting unsnagged, pulling this way and that and swearing "damn" in a gruff way but today she couldn't and her dad had to grab the rod and do it himself. He pulled and pulled, impatient with her for getting snagged in the first place. He gave it a last, mighty pull. The red devil tore loose, shot up out of the water in a flash of light and one of the big treble hooks sank deep into the back of her father's hand.

He yelled, he swore, he stomped both his feet while hunched over, a weird marching on the spot, protective of his hand, cradling it with the other, while holding tight to the lure so it didn't wobble and jerk and hurt him more.

"*Jesus.*"

"Is it okay?"

"*God damn it.*"

Val asked if she could help and when she approached he turned his back on her in case she tried to touch it. Those barbs on the hooks sure worked, she thought. It was amazing anyone ever lost a hooked fish.

He told her to get his fishing knife from the tackle box. She found it buried under stinky bait jars and a crusted rag. It was actually more hunting knife than fishing knife, according to him. It wasn't very sharp. She had cleaned two perch with it last time and it still looked dirty from that and she could even smell it. She was careful to pass the knife properly, handle pointed away, and her father took it from her without looking at her. He tried gingerly nicking enough skin to free the hook. He stopped and swore and looked up and glared out across the land, which was hazy with summer heat. He put his head down to try again, but he couldn't bring himself to make the slice that would do the job.

"You do it." He thrust the knife her way, point first.

He pulled steadily on the lure so a taut tent of skin pulled up away from the bones.

"Do it fast."

Val knew the knife was sharpest closest to the handle, as dull knives often are, and when she positioned that part over the stretched skin he asked her what she thought she was doing and she explained. He said nothing. He closed his eyes. A semi whooshed by and honked long but neither of them moved. If ever there was a perfect time for a slug of whiskey and a leather belt to bite, this was it, thought Val, and she would never see a Hollywood bullet extraction without thinking of this scene on the Brokenhead River bridge.

It was hard cutting into a father's flesh with a dirty knife. Her careful sawing made him wince and grit his teeth and finally shout, *Just do it*. She actually expected him to hit her. She gritted her own teeth and for some reason shouted those same words then put muscle into it, gouging. Out the hook popped, followed by a rush of his blood.

He didn't congratulate or thank her. He found a bandaid in the tackle box and they kept fishing. It looked like he picked up pace on the beer.

She liked his silence and anger even less now and in any case she'd earned the right to leave him. She went down the bank and around a first bend in the river behind some trees, out of sight of the bridge and her father, which made it a bit scary, but also a joy. Here was a grassy clearing, cool in the shade. A few old lure packages told her that others fished here. It was so wonderfully cool it made her picture her hot, squinting father, but she chased that thought away. With a sharp rock she dug up a worm and affixed it wriggling to two of the treble hooks, and when she cast the red devil twenty feet straight in front of her it wasn't in the water five seconds before a giant golden fish leapt up thrashing. She knew right away it was a great big carp.

It was the best fish-fight of her life, though this is partly because she would rarely fish again. It was five or six pounds, and carp do put up a tussle. She held her breath the whole time, especially when it jumped, and at some point she yelled for her father, or perhaps she simply screamed. He arrived just as she was getting it up onto the bank. She knelt admiring and petting it and her father said it was time to pack up and go home. The huge scales were a burnished gold. It had a startling smell, like mud but sweet. Her dad said carp were too bony to eat, throw it back. She insisted on taking it. He made her put it in the trunk, wrapped in old newspaper she hurried to find under the bridge. The ride home was quiet and it was the last time they fished the Brokenhead River.

For some reason she was forbidden to cook the carp at home though she often cooked their catch and even her father said she was good at it. Not telling her parents, she took the fish across the street to Mark's house. Mark was two years older, so they weren't exactly friends, but he fired up his family barbeque. Mark's parents were out for the evening and they'd left him with a TV dinner, the one where the apple crumble dessert bubbles and bleeds over into the compartment of corn. Val proudly beheaded and gutted the carp in Mark's kitchen sink, and they made a tray out of tin foil. He told her it was expensive but she went ahead and put five dollops of butter on it—Mark found her use of "dollops" extremely funny—which gradually melted as the fish sizzled over the coals. When it was done, she lifted the knob of the severed backbone and it rose free of the tender flesh, trailed by a perfect skeleton of artfully symmetrical little bones. The meat was white and smelled like a pond. She squeezed lemon, *then* the salt. If you do it the other way, she instructed Mark as he watched her work, the lemon washes the salt off. She ran across the street for some parsley secreted from a neighbour's garden, right under their kitchen window.

Val and Mark sat down facing each other, which was proper. She insisted on napkins. She ate a ton of carp, twice as much as Mark did. It tasted better even than pickerel, or fresh mahi mahi when she would one day taste that, and no one would ever convince her otherwise.

At the end of the meal she stood up, walked round the table to Mark's side, bent down and, clumsy, surprising him completely and most likely frightening him as well, kissed him on the lips, keeping her mouth closed. And then, though she knew he wouldn't know how to do it either, she made Mark have something like sex with her.

•

THE CAPERS WERE PROPERLY NOT IN THE SAUCE AFTER ALL, but employed visually, riding the edge of sauce like a bas-relief dotted line. It added an element that approached humour. Probably the word was "play." It seemed to be the chef's signature. In any case, the carp in black butter proved delicious, nothing like lard from a hairbrush, not a bone, and no sign of tweezer marks. Lee liked his taste of carp too, though he preferred his duck—he always did, he loved duck—and she suspected he couldn't taste her subtle fish properly because of the harsh cassis that coated his duck skin almost purple. She tasted it, but appearance alone would earn it negative mention. With Chinese food, well, maybe, but with French a sauce should never overcrow a flesh. She didn't know how the review would go. The food here was almost excellent, but the word "almost" held a world of flaws.

They were having a small argument, over the wine, which was also excellent. The hipster waiter, who she decided she liked, had come through with a superb California Pinot. When he finished pouring them each a glass, he said, simply, making her recall the big scene in that movie, "And now you can have the best talk of your life."

But first they argued, a little. Clinking glasses, Lee said, nodding at his wine, "I'll try to catch up with you."

"What do you mean?"

"I mean, glug-glug, I'll try to catch up."

"Are you saying I've had more than you?"

He simply shrugged by way of answering.

"I'm pretty sure it's the other way around."

"I don't think so."

"It's always the other way around."

Lee didn't appear to like this one much, but all he said was, "Okay sure maybe, but not tonight."

Bringing this next wine to her lips, she only had to feel within for a moment, her warm core, to know he was right. She was a little drunk. That carp had made her nervous. Maybe "nervous" wasn't the word. She never knew what the word was when she thought about her father.

She snorted. Lee was quick to smile. "What?"

Val had just told herself a joke. It was, He's been dead almost fifteen years and he still doesn't love me.

"Nothing," she said. "I was thinking about wine, I was thinking that this one was a bit too smoky, and then I thought, 'How in hell can *any*body say *any*thing bad about good wine?'"

"Well exactly!"

They clinked glasses again, and Lee drank deeply, unabashedly catching up. So Val drank deep too, mischievously keeping ahead. Lee saw this and laughed and glugged again, and so did she, until laughter stopped them, and they didn't say a word, they knew each other this well. The waiter was at their side now, looking from one to the other with stage-concern, in on their joke whatever it might be.

Maybe this restaurant was simply excellent. Really, who would know or care? She wondered if she was possibly getting soft. But who cared about that either?

They ordered dessert and coffee, and considered the wisdom of another drink. Deciding, Lee flagged the waiter for two Calvados. Doubles, please. When the waiter said, "Oo, can I watch?" Lee laughed for him and Val didn't. When lines were crossed it sometimes earned a mention. It didn't help when, as the waiter withdrew, Lee pointed out the blotch of wine-dribble on the shoulder of her blouse.

"A good frenzy," she said and eyed him in a way that could be sexual if he wanted it to be.

Lee poured what remained of the wine into their glasses, and told her why this was a special occasion. It came out in a crude tumble, Lee boyishly nervous.

What he said first was, "I want you to come to China with me."

She made her "okaaay" sound nothing like agreement but "say more."

He did. He was going to China, mostly Shanghai, but also Hong Kong, and the project would last possibly two weeks, depending on Hong Kong, but since they'd already be there they could then travel a bit, maybe to those beaches in Thailand, where he was amazed he'd never been, and maybe Australia, "since we'll be in the general area," though he had no idea why she'd want to go to Australia. In fact, what was he thinking, stupid of him.

"How do you know I wouldn't want to go to Australia?" Valerie disliked this kind of assumption even more than the assumption that she would want to travel, live, and share a hotel room and its glaring bed, for weeks.

"Well, the food," Lee said.

Or the assumption that she didn't work for a living, didn't have her job to do.

"What about my work?" She met and held his eyes. She knew he wanted to proclaim that she wouldn't have to spend a penny.

"Another book." He shrugged as though this were obvious. He'd thought this through. He smiled wider, more whitely, hideously. "I'll be away lots, I'll zip down to Hong Kong, you go wild in Shanghai. I hear it's fusion city."

She cut right to it.

"Why would we sleep together there, when we don't sleep together here?"

He was ready for this too. He laid his arm flat on the table, palm up, asking for her hand to join his. "Well, why don't we sleep together here?"

Their desserts came at this of all times and she didn't have to decide whether, fatally, to lay her hand in his.

He had a standard crème brûlée, with the nod to Asia some ginger fibres spiderwebbing the caramelized crust. Her dessert was one of the oddest she'd ever encountered. It entirely lacked any actual sweetness, being comprised of slivers of toasted almond and raw garlic coated with unsweetened ginger chocolate.

She began eating hers. After a long pause, head down, so did Lee.

She'd once had an equally unsweet dessert, a sorbet made from rosemary and rose petal and lime, no added sweetener, and it was bizarre how, in forcing the tongue to seek sweetness, the tongue somehow found it, or at least flavours that hinted at it. Tonight's dessert, lumpy and brown-black and looking rather fecal in its white bowl, climaxed in an odd savoury spike, almost a sweetness, in the garlic itself.

"What about Klaatu?" Valerie said.

"What *about* Klaatu?"

"What will you do with it?"

"She'll be happy at a friend's. She'll be all fat when we get back."

He shouldn't have said we. He just shouldn't have.

"No."

"No?" He looked away and swallowed. "Just no?" He pushed aside his half-eaten dessert, shaking his head minutely. "I mean, you didn't have to give me an answer right away." He tried smiling. "Especially that one."

Valerie almost said "yes" then, she was that drunk. And she might have meant it. There was a sloppiness in all of this that was dangerous, she could see at least that clearly. From his posture she understood the immensity of his proposition, that he had his sights set on the largest view, on this trip as a test for a future together. His face was that serious. So she had misread this man for almost two years, misread his way with her as happy ease.

"Maybe," Lee said, trying not to be plaintive, smiling enough to show the tips of his white teeth, "you'd like some time to think?"

Val knew her smile was coy, cold even, though all she felt was paralyzed. She managed to pick up her spoon, hold it a foot away, turn its bowl to her face and do her little fish-eye mirror thing with it. And here she was again, her face contained and made ridiculous, the nose outsized and bulbous. She tilted the spoon, and her eyes moved away, tiny with incomprehension and yearning while her chin became a moronic club. She'd been studying this face for decades.

She put down her spoon. Lee. Christ. It was Lee. Fuck. She knew that this might be the last time an offer like this was made to her by anyone. And that that should in no way matter to her. But it did. It did now. Perhaps, when you near fifty, a thing like integrity is allowed to molt, and become something else. Something smaller and blinking and with unformed taste.

Valerie examined her hesitation, her simple breathing. Her remaining privacy. She said to Lee, "I don't need more time."

His stare was as pure as a dog's, waiting to see if food would appear, or not.

She asked him, "So, when?"

Lee's eyes were nothing now but happy, and invited everything within her. This was almost good enough.

DRILLING A HOLE IN YOUR BOAT

THIS BEAUTIFUL MORNING YOU'VE ARRANGED TO MEET THE mechanic at the marina. The engine has been failing to start. From atop the ramp you can see over to your slip where *Sylvan* is moored, and there's Marty already aboard and at work. The bay is calm and you're struck by how the boats ride such water. All the white hulls. The sailboat masts more still than trees. It's like the boats are alert, more than any land-bound thing.

You walk the dock head down, wondering how this will go. At the boat, his back is to you so you say hi. Despite what's on your mind it's unnerving to greet him—Marty looks *exactly* like Richard Dreyfuss, circa age thirty-five. A pudgier version but so identical that the start of any conversation startles you to hear the wrong voice come out. Instead of attending the words, you wonder why Richard Dreyfuss is dropping his *g*'s and how he knows so much about engines, and when it was he moved here to the island. Maybe it's all for an upcoming role?

Marty is already greasy to the elbows and has uncoiled a length of red electrical wire along the deck. You carry a load of bottled water and two folded blankets. Essentials. You keep them visible and then purposely drop a bottle loud on the dock so Marty will all the more likely remember seeing them if he is asked. Someone out to deliberately sink his boat would not bring nice blankets or a supply of water. You wonder who will be doing the asking. Coast Guard, police, insurance adjuster. All of them? The word for deliberately sinking a boat is *scuttle*, and though none of them will use the term, because you'll make sure they have no reason to, you still don't like it. *Scuttle* lacks the nobility, and the melancholy, of something beautiful sinking out of sight.

"Found your ignition problem," Marty says. Richard Dreyfuss. You inwardly startle again.

"Great. Good."

"You didn't have the starter wire tight to the bolt and it didn't like that."

"Ahh. Okay." You don't appreciate the *you* slant in his sentence because it was *he* who didn't tighten that wire to the bolt two years back when he installed that starter in the first place. But you like Marty, he does decent work and specializes in exactly the old engine model you have. You believe he could fix it eyes closed—in effect he does, you've seen him lying half in the open hatch with arms around it, cheek pressed to the cold and rust, blind hands feeling around for wires and bolts. Maybe he took up marine engine repair right after *Jaws*.

Marty deliberately does not pause in stripping wire as he mumbles, "Got my divorce papers served today."

And he will come fix your boat the morning he gets served divorce papers.

"Wow." You don't know what else to say just yet.

"Guy comes right to the door. One way to ruin your breakfast, that's for sure."

"That's hard."

"Woulda smacked him if I was still drinkin'. Woulda chased him down the road." He looks up at you. "*Big* time."

"Well yeah."

You tell him you appreciate him fixing your boat under the circumstances, and mention again the trip you're embarking on this evening. Egmont draws a blank look so you explain that Egmont is an hour up past Pender Harbour.

"You guys'll like Pender," he says. "It's nice up there."

You wonder why he assumes you don't know Pender Harbour when you just said your destination was an even smaller place beyond it. But you do know why he assumes your wife is coming along. Getting divorced, he naturally imagines everyone else taking cozy trips with loving wives. His assumption is natural also because people generally don't make voyages solo. Lots of people around here don't even fish alone. Gales come up. Rogue waves. Things can happen. You picture your cordless drill wrapped in a piece of old carpet and stowed in a hatch under the bow. You secreted it on board two nights ago, in the dark. You were desperate that night, not thinking straight. Hyperventilating and wanting to just do it, go back to the house and get Julie, just roll the dice and risk them finding out what you'd done. But you tested the motor and it wouldn't start. You went home, took one of Julie's Dilaudid, stopped hyperventilating, thought things through. Your plan became an actual plan. It began to look good. Almost like a healthy answer to a sickening problem, even a problem the size of lives. Your plan feels so good now that you can find the faint breeze of humour again. For instance, here's a movie star fixing a boat you're going to sink.

As Dreyfuss stands on deck, not quite looking at the wire as he crimps off another half-inch, you spend the next ten minutes hearing about Marty's wife and thirteen-year-old daughter. You learn Marty has been on the wagon for ten years while his wife's drinking has grown worse. Custody is going to be battled in court. He's tried and tried to get her to stop drinking. Both her parents are alcoholics, just as on his side, his father and a brother, who's "doing hard time" in South Dakota, of all places. You've never pictured a prison in South Dakota but for some reason it's easy. A grey monolith surrounded by treeless wastes. Possibly you'll be in a prison if you somehow get caught surviving this. You can write *A Mariner's Guide to Self Sabotage*.

Over Dreyfuss's shoulder you can see through the harbour mouth. The strait is windless and glassy. A little beyond what you can see, it's over one thousand feet deep. Beckoning, a final safe haven. You're listening to Marty, you're patient. You wish you could feel for him. And then you do. When he first got going on his divorce thing you wanted to tell him to please just fix the boat, everyone has problems, in fact some problems make his look puny, but you understand again that pain is pain, and while he has his way of trying to feel better—talking about it—you have yours—drilling a hole in your boat.

"Alcohol," he looks up at you to make sure you're listening to this part, "makes you crazy." You are listening, so he widens his eyes and shakes his head, and then a little Dreyfuss chuckle. "Completely crazy." He drops his head. "And I've stopped bein' fuckin' polite about it."

So he'll know that you understand, you slip in that you had this affliction in your family too, your father, though you see your ulterior motive is to suggest that it's a common thing and maybe get him to stop talking and get down to work. He makes no sign he heard you; he explains that the only nights his wife doesn't get shitfaced is when she's too wasted from being shitfaced the night before. You start to bristle again and look away, but when he moans that his daughter has "grown up thinking crazy is normal" you feel his genuine sadness, and you think of Christine. You want to share that you also have a daughter who probably thinks crazy is normal, who is depressed and poor and uncommunicative in a distant big city. But you keep still, and stomach the helplessness of fathers who have daughters living out of reach.

Richard Dreyfuss bends for a roll of electrical tape and the boat dips almost imperceptibly, but enough to distress Julie's lost sense of balance if she were sitting here in her chair. You can see her panic and grab the gunnel, then laugh at herself, laughing at something else that is new. You picture her sitting here unflinchingly, despite her vast pain, listening to Marty's story with nothing but empathy. She would listen with perfect patience and say not just the right things but helpful things, and make Marty feel better about himself. You think about Julie's life ending and understand for maybe the first time that her empathy is a force very much alive in the world, and that it will also end. You wonder again if she knows what you're up to. You won't ask her. You are almost certain she would be with you in this, with you all the way, but you know you won't dare ask.

Marty is describing a recent fishing trip with his daughter. Shaking his head and smiling he says, "She can take an hour of fishing at most," and you're pretty sure that she was dead bored out there alone with Dad, and that Dad can't see this or admit it to himself. You stare over his shoulder at the pure windlessness of the broad strait, a glass dome on the infinite calm beneath.

And then return to the image of this evening when you will wheel Julie down that ramp, walking backwards, leading her chair, slowing for the bumps to soften them, then stopping at this old fibreglass boat, named *Sylvan*, as if it were a product of the forest, like the old ships, though the only wood on *Sylvan* is a bit of teak trim, worn grey and in need of stain. Julie will comment that she hasn't been on the boat in almost a year. You lift her in your arms and climb aboard with her, trying not to be devastated by her thinness, her shocking insubstantiality, a rib cage so crushable, those knees the widest things below her hips. No, before you lift her she'll pause to consider the process of boarding *Sylvan*, the coming pain of it. She'll tap her patch, going "Doink, doink, doink," to lighten things. Then slur a soft "damn" as she blurs out. She doesn't want to blur out, these days. She doesn't want to sleep. You announce to yourself, again, what has to be the truth: she wants to die, but she doesn't want to sleep, and they are different things.

She's doped up so vague on your gimpy leg as you hoist her over the gunnel. She smiles, jokes sleepily about you dropping her, asking how high you think she'd bounce. Last year, she adds, she would have bounced just fine. She's wrapped in her soft grey blanket and wearing one of her toques. The red one. Red fails to outdo her face, even now, she's that striking. She'll smile about this evening boat ride they're taking, call him a romantic. You'll wonder again if she knows. She's so good at secrets, better than you are. It's never been possible to know her fully, and you know that this has been best, because it has worked perfectly for you both. Julie looks good in that toque. She looks great in any hat you put on her. That smile still comes easily, despite all. This morning she launched a good snort when you told her Richard Dreyfuss had retired and was fixing their boat.

That laugh of hers is so beautiful. It always has a reason.

There's a gap in Marty's talking as he studies the exposed wire, like he's unsure about it. Maybe he's insulted, maybe he saw you way off in your head, not listening. You hear yourself propose that he must be worried about his daughter, seeing how she has the genes from both sides of the family, and he shakes his head vehemently. No, she really has it together, he says. You almost say that high school and boys and parties—a.k.a. booze—haven't begun to hammer on her yet, and that it might not be pretty, especially with a mother whose normal is crazy, but you keep mum. Marty is sufficiently upset about those papers on his kitchen counter.

You can't help but smile to picture your daughter getting the news. You have no idea how she'll react. You suspect she'll guess the truth. She might know instantly, every bit of it. Which is part of your pleasure. You and Christine have never been close, yet you have always been able to read each other despite not necessarily wanting to. Even while she was growing up, the ways you bothered each other were obvious yet incomprehensible to you both.

Last month when you flew Christine home for a probable last visit with her mother, she could hardly look at let alone speak to Julie, and she barely acknowledged you at all. Christine was suffering the most. Her whole life, from the very beginning it seems, her love for both of you has been complex, her face a peeved unvoiced question. Only Julie was able to soothe her, make her smile, and you admit you've been jealous of this, while at the same time grateful that your daughter had at least one of you. But for the entire week of her visit, Christine barely ate and did not shower and her hair turned sleekly metallic. It was so extreme—her pain as revealed by her dismal hair—that it became almost funny. Unable to attend to pain other than her own, Julie did manage a stage-whisper to you, "Get that girl an *aspirin*." It got so that whatever humour Christine might still find in her life disappeared completely, so much so that her mother's quiet joking, and even more so yours, threw her into a rage. When that TV show ended and you asked Julie to please just get over herself and carry you to bed, good God, Christine's eyes rammed shut and she shuddered with what looked like hatred. She was suffering the fact of a dying mother, but also a useless father, and it was more than she could take. It was clear that she would suffer less without them.

Life-sized problems can be fixed sometimes.

Marty has finished his story and has simply turned away from you, getting on with the job. You tried to listen, you did. You are just not as good as some people.

You go below with the blankets and water. Like the drill, other supplies are stowed and waiting. You open the tiny fridge to check the treats you two can nibble while you leisurely motor out to a thousand feet. Plums and apples from your own trees, three of each. (You wonder why three. Maybe in some way you are wanting to include Christine in the voyage?) A square of beautiful white cheddar, wrapped in paper, tied with string. An expensive gypsy sausage you remember Julie once moaned over as she gnawed some right from the package.

In a dry-bag on the berth cushion there's a change of clothes for you both. Two fluffy pillows, twist-tied in garbage bags, meaning they will float. You've planned flotsam as evidence. You eye the kitchen leftovers containers snapped shut, a rubberized overnight bag, an empty propane canister with *Sylvan* sharpied on, another cooler, some cushions—all things to bob about and be found, alerting authorities. Things suggesting a journey. Even a whiff of suicide, you learned, negates your life insurance.

You find yourself gazing at the insides of a hapless boat which is now also at the end of its life. *Sylvan* was built in the sixties, old for a boat, especially one not that well cared for. You take in its homely bones. For some reason you feel nostalgia for its defects especially. The heater that doesn't work. The step-down that's wobbly. The tiny sink and faucet. The lumpy V-berth. The smallest bathroom possible, and so ludicrously close to the berth that you hear each other's tinkle as if amplified, as if an inch away. In eight years of having *Sylvan*, you've spent three weekends aboard with Julie, and none for several years. You've made love exactly four times in here—once interrupting an afternoon's fishing just as they were starting to bite. "So you don't like fishing *that* much," becoming one of her in-jokes with you.

You don't love this boat like you've seen others love their boats, but you're fond enough, especially now. That it floats at all, that you're standing on water, is a kind of magic. It's a worthy vessel for tonight's cruise. It's better than a hospital bed. You see how it's better because it's what you've chosen. Choice being better, so much better, than no choice.

As if to join the commentary on your boat, Richard Dreyfuss appears at the top of the step, inclines his head in. "Hey, you know your radio doesn't work."

"Really!"

You had spent time on it, locating the main wire to the antenna and then scraping at it with a file till it broke. You couldn't just snip it because it would look deliberate. Mostly, you didn't want to find yourself halfway into the process of sinking, panicking knee-deep in cold water and sending out a mayday.

Marty says, unapologetically, "I wanted to check the weather. Looked almost like something chewed through it. I did a quick splice, so it works now." He won't look at you, but this can't possibly be out of suspicion. He's just disgusted with you as a sailor in general.

"Thanks," you say. "Phew."

"That radio's bad anyway. Get a new one. Seriously."

"I will."

You begin imagining how authorities will interpret things now, having received no distress call despite—and confirmed by the local marine mechanic—the missing vessel having an operational radio.

"I mean," says Marty, "it's okay to have a beater-boat but the safety gear needs to be good."

"Well, I agree."

"How are your flares?"

"They're good, they're good." You're nervous now. You don't like this line of talk. You did check the flares and they did look okay. The plan is to fire them all into the water some time well into the sinking. They might be found, charred and floating, irrefutable evidence of trying to be saved, nothing suicidal in this event whatsoever. But why would someone set off flares yet not radio for help? Maybe you could wait until the very, very last, just before the radio itself is submerged? And only then call a mayday? But you've planned to be at peace, immobile and glowing with Dilaudid. You've planned for Julie to be perfectly out of it too, you won't for one second want to disturb her last living dreams with badly acted shouts of "mayday!" Even worse, maybe the boat, which isn't very heavy as boats go, maybe the boat will sink slowly, too slowly after the last-minute distress call, maybe it would hesitate forever in its final going down and the Coast Guard would actually appear and save you both, and see everything that you've done. What next for Julie, then.

You turn away, not wanting Marty to see your face. You hear him retreat and stomp around back up on deck, gathering tools. He did say the radio was "bad." Maybe he'll remember that, and maybe that's what he'll tell them when they ask him his thoughts about the mystery of no distress call. You try to calm down. You feel the furtiveness of your glance out the porthole.

Tonight will work. Will play out. Will fix everything.

It's funny that what you're using to fix things is an actual tool. A cordless drill. You've never owned a cordless before, though you've felt some envy watching workers use them, free of electricity, whipping them from their belts like pistols. It cost forty-nine dollars at a hardware store. Two towns over, and you paid cash. And wore sunglasses, which made you snicker to catch sight of yourself in the window on your way in. The law left you no choice, really. No one can help someone end it, not even in a case as deeply right as yours. You go to jail. Julie would never let you risk that. So she sacrifices herself, she suffers her hell, she stifles what gasps and groans she can in hopes that you won't put yourself in jeopardy. Well, you've pulled a little switcheroo on her, haven't you?

This evening will be calm and perfect. You open the fridge again and poke the cheese with a finger, testing for coolness. You catch yourself and stop. The taste of cheddar, the calmness of an evening, even the godliness of a sunset—it just doesn't count any more. Who cares what the last hours are like? This old boat will soon be wedged in mud in darkness a thousand feet deep. In mud for as long as fibreglass lasts. The only possible perfection left is that soon it will all be over. Nothing else counts. Your bodies, your bones, you find you can think of them scientifically now, which is a relief, there's no dismay as you picture them inert, picked clean, on the bottom, dull white except that there isn't enough light down there for them to be white or anything else, though Julie's are easier to imagine, still wrapped in her nylon windbreaker and pants, and not much thinner than her body is already. It's also painless to see your bones burning up in crematory fire if it happens that you've floated to the surface and are found. You wonder what Christine would prefer. That is, what would hurt her the least? Probably two parents floated up, and found. But it would have to be both. Not just one. And certainly not just him.

Now you imagine that other question for Christine. The biggest one. It almost makes you laugh. It would be too cruel ever to ask it. But what future would your daughter choose, if given the choice? Would she choose ten more years of a sole surviving parent, a widower father for whom she feels mostly a chafing ambivalence and who lives three thousand miles away, or would she choose a fast two million dollars? What a question! You feel cruel even thinking such a thing.

You wonder how she'll use it. If she'll spend it wisely. You hope she'll have the strength. Especially if—not if, when—that last guy, Joey, hears the news of her good fortune and comes sniffing around. But money certainly isn't everything. Her happiness is not guaranteed and there's no point in pretending it is. Mostly this feels like a simple, possible good thing, some kind of fresh start, to give her.

Almost like the boat itself decides to, the engine cranks and roars to life. Then shuts off. Then starts again. And one more time. Richard Dreyfuss has fixed the ignition problem.

"Hey!"

Marty is summoning you, you think impolitely given your age difference, but you realize he might not remember your name.

"Hey," he calls again. "It's done."

You pop back up on deck, hand in your back pocket for your chequebook. You want to pay him twice what he's earned, three times, because why wouldn't you, but it would be suspicious.

You congratulate and thank Marty for his work. Now he magically remembers a phone message you left "quite a ways back." It was a full year ago, actually, but he asks you if the engine is still overheating. It still very much is, but you tell him no. He looks at you dubiously, ready to sprout that little Dreyfuss smirk. You expect a quip about you cheating on him with another mechanic, or did the engine just get better on its own. But then he tells you that you can fix the overheating yourself.

"Get a toothpick," he says, "jump in the water and dig out the intake there on the leg. Little slits right in front of the prop." He hooks his thumb over his shoulder, indicating the back of the boat. "Late August, there's mussels and crap growing there in your slits, guaranteed."

"Okay. Sounds good," you nod, wondering if he's putting you on. Crap in your slits, well okay. You're thirty years older than him and you limp. You won't be jumping in any ocean to fix your engine with a toothpick. What does Richard Dreyfuss know about boats, anyway? Though he *was* the only one to survive that shark.

You'll tell her about Dreyfuss when you get home. But Julie should be here for this. Laughing really isn't the same when it's just you.

I'D LIKE TO THANK THE BC ARTS COUNCIL FOR ITS SUPPORT. Also to Shed and Nicola and to the fine folks at Douglas & McIntyre for taking a chance on these stories, and to Barbara Berson for her fine eye. And thanks, as always, to my agent, Carolyn Forde.

I'd like to thank the editors of *The New Quarterly*, *The Malahat Review*, *The Fiddlehead*, and *Zoetrope: All-Story*.

And, in no particular order, thanks to those who read or helped or prompted: Janice McCachen, Graydon Tait, DW Wilson, Lee Henderson, Brian Guns, Joan MacLeod, Dede Crane, John Gould and Lise Gaston.